Return To
PORTER'S HOLLOW

Yvonne Schuchart

ISBN 13: 978-1-945670-46-6
ISBN 10: 1-945670-46-0

Year of the Book
135 Glen Avenue
Glen Rock, PA 17327

Library of Congress Control Number: 2017955422

DEDICATION

This book is dedicated to you, the reader,

because let's face it, a book is useless if no one reads it.

Yvonne
Schuchart
12/2/17

ACKNOWLEDGMENTS

I can hardly believe it! Here I am again at the release of another book. So thankful to the powers that be for another year to write, and live, and write...

I need to thank Earl Schuchart, my significant other, who since the release of my last book has become my husband. He's always in my corner encouraging me to believe in myself, and I certainly wouldn't want to disappoint him.

A loud, resounding thank you to Demi Stevens of Year of the Book for her input, editing, coaching, teaching, cheerleading, and most of all her friendship. Without her, this book wouldn't be in your hands right now.

Thank you also to Kimberly Albert and Cynthia Hospador for taking the time to proofread this book and help tidy up the details.

And I always appreciate everyone in my writer's groups for their helpful comments, tips, and encouragement. Again, I couldn't have done this without all of them.

And finally, thank you, reader, for your time.

*"Home is the place where when you go there,
you have to finally face the thing in the dark."*
-Stephen King, *It*, 1986

PROLOGUE

Fine sight to see. Laura Allen standing by the very gravestone Curry had put there years ago himself. Crying like this wasn't all her fault in the first place. The way he saw it, if she hadn't found Lottie Edwards' body all those years ago, none of this would've happened.

Women were evil. That's all there was to it. They used their eyes on a man the way Delilah used her scissors on Samson's hair. Drained the will right out of him, took his soul. Curry hated their eyes.

And now hers were leaking like she'd lost everything. "Hmmph, pluck 'em right out of her head. That's what'll fix it."

He caught movement to the side of the group by the grave. Loy stood there with his hand over his eyes, looking straight at Curry.

He slipped into the woods then and made his way back to his new home—in the caves beyond Porter's Hollow.

Laura watched Blaine Wilson climb the steps to the porch and take the cup she reached out to him. There was something about this man's presence that was exhilarating and discomfiting at the same time.

He sat in the rocking chair quietly for several minutes as he studied his cup intently. Suddenly he turned his head toward her and broke the silence.

"I suppose you'll be visiting your Aunt Hattie often?" he asked.

Laura smiled and nodded, "I hope to."

He clamped his lips shut and turned his attention back to the coffee. Laura watched him, wanting to speak up. Her heart pounded in her ears. She'd lost the moment.

"Just remember. Leave the search for murderers and villains to me." He stood and downed the rest of his coffee in one gulp, then handed her the empty cup.

Robey came out onto the porch.

"You ladies have a safe trip home," he said, acknowledging Laura and her mother.

Blaine descended the steps with his hat still in hand. He turned at the bottom and nodded to them both. But he looked directly at Laura—and finally smiled—as he gave her that familiar two-fingered salute.

CHAPTER 1

Jacobus, PA
Saturday, October 30, 2010

Laura Evans bent down on one knee to retie her hiking boot. She was on a trail in William Cain County Park that meandered through woodlands along the edge of Lake Redman, about a half mile from her home. A peaceful, quiet place to think and plan.

A flash of pale blue caught her eye, out of place among the browns and yellows of mid-autumn. A late morning fog swirled around a young girl as she stepped onto the path wearing only a thin dress, white bobby socks, and black patent leather shoes. What on earth was a child doing out here dressed in summer clothes?

Something dark and sticky ran down the side of the girl's face—*blood!* Her blonde hair hung damp and disheveled, in her bright blue eyes shone a silent plea.

Laura stood up cautiously as the child turned her way. *It can't be!* She rubbed her scrunched eyes and opened them again. *It's not possible. Lottie Edwards?*

Lottie had haunted Laura's dreams for a time, but those dreams had stopped once Laura discovered the truth surrounding Lottie's death. What could the child possibly want from her now? And this time was different—Laura was wide awake. Yet Lottie stood there, as real as the bright red and yellow sassafras trees along the path.

Laura held her breath, heart throbbing in her throat as Lottie mouthed the words, *Come—please—come back.* Then the girl turned away, heading down the trail, and the woods around them began to change. At last Laura's own limbs responded and she followed. A heavy grey-blue mist swirled, and their footfalls made no sound on the soft dirt.

The path became a steep rutted dirt road, twisting upward toward a cluster of tall pine trees. Laura recognized the lane as the one that ran up into the mountain above Porter's Hollow—in North Carolina.

She followed Lottie, not quite able to close the distance between them. The twilight haze surrounding them disoriented Laura, but she recognized the old Hadley cabin. Still the child went on, farther and farther into the woods. The path ended at a steep rocky outcrop. Finally, the girl stopped and turned to face Laura, brows furrowed, eyes imploring. She mouthed again, *"Please come back."* Then she climbed to the edge of the rocks.

Panic seized Laura, though it didn't make any sense. She couldn't save the child. The little girl with Down Syndrome had died years ago, raped by Laura's Uncle Curry, and murdered by Laura's own father. Glen Porter had confessed to all of it, right before he died. Yet, the truth hadn't set anyone free.

Still, watching Lottie poised on the edge of the cliff, Laura wanted to run, but her limbs were so heavy. Lottie was too close...

"No!" Laura screamed. Finally her legs broke free and she ran, but it was too late. Lottie jumped.

Laura slid to a stop at the overhang, frantically searching the ground below for the girl, but she'd disappeared.

Laura backed away, tearing her gaze from the cliff edge. She turned and stumbled, falling onto her hands and knees, back on the trail beside Lake Redman. Not more than ten yards away from where she'd been hiking.

She scrambled to her feet, looking in every direction, but the child was gone. Laura shivered and her breath came out in hard white puffs, rising around her face. She checked her watch and her eyebrows shot up. Only five minutes had passed. She peered over her shoulder with a self-conscious blush, then hurried along the trail, forcing herself not to run, squaring her shoulders to ward off the growing sense of panic.

She reached the road to the development beyond the park and stopped. Leaning down, both hands on her knees, head hung low, she worked to slow her breathing. Several seconds later she set out again, but her mind churned as she rounded the corner onto her block. The vision, or whatever it was, had been so real—but she wasn't one to put much stock in the psychic, or the paranormal. At least, she'd never thought herself susceptible to all that mumbo jumbo. Still, the dreams had turned out to be true. She and Lottie were linked in a way. Maybe it wasn't such a big jump to actually experience the supernatural.

The mailman reached Laura's box as she turned into her driveway. "Morning," he said.

"Good morning." She managed the reply, still breathless, her hands shaking as she reached for the stack of what looked like mostly junk mail he'd rubber banded.

"Selling the place?" He pointed to the realtor's sign in her yard.

She took a steadying breath before responding. "Yeah, it's time."

"Sorry to see you go. You and Doug were good neighbors." He dropped his head, leafing through the mail. "I mean your husband was a good... you know what I mean."

Laura smiled and thanked him. People still fumbled when they acknowledged Doug's death. She knew what it was like to be on both sides of the issue, but she'd reached a place she could forgive others their awkward sympathies.

Laura turned away, stopping as she neared the house to survey the brick, split rancher where she'd spent the better part of her life. So many memories to sort through and pack away, so much living to put in order, so much bitter and sweet to sift and savor, but those things were only part of the reason the decision to sell was so difficult.

Her home was the most concrete part of the marriage she had left, the most solid, real part of Doug that remained. They'd had so many good years, despite how distant they'd grown in the last few. She could almost hear him telling her not to be hasty. If such a decision was up to him, he'd probably stretch the thing out forever. She gave a sad smile at all the times she'd given in to his preferences. But this time she'd made a decision on her own and she was not turning back.

She would miss living in rural Pennsylvania, but winter was coming on and the heating bills and taxes were high. She didn't want to deplete her savings by using it to supplement regular bills. There were solid reasons she'd chosen to go through with the sale.

Now boxes cluttered every room. No way she could show it in such a state, and her first appointment was Monday. To top it off, Thanksgiving was only three and a half weeks away, and she was supposed to go to North Carolina to her great Aunt Hattie's. Laura chided herself for the poor timing. She should've skipped her weekend hike this morning, but it usually kept her sane, helped her refocus.

In the kitchen, Laura poured a large mug of coffee, taking a quick peek over her shoulder and around the room. Half expecting to see—what? Ghosts?

She pulled the rubber band off the stack of mail. Among the advertising fliers and bills was a formal, business sized envelope from Hannah's Hope House. Laura plopped onto a kitchen chair and slit the envelope open, holding her breath as she read the letter. *A written employment warning.*

She'd left her supervisor at Hannah's in the lurch when she went to North Carolina on such short notice a few weeks ago. Then she'd compounded the problem by staying longer than promised.

Laura's face warmed with guilt. Even if she didn't agree with everything the woman said, or the way she said it in the letter, Shelly was right to be upset.

Working with special needs clients was stressful and it took everyone pulling together to keep things manageable. Laura knew that better than most. Her own little girl with Down Syndrome had only lived to be five. She had worked so hard to teach her to communicate, to take care of bathroom habits, to control erratic behavior. It was a bittersweet strain she'd never forget, and it was the reason she'd chosen this line of work.

She rifled through the rest of the mail and came across a small envelope in the middle of the stack with no return address. She didn't recognize the thin scrawling print, but it was postmarked from West Jefferson, North Carolina.

The single piece of white paper inside read: *You comin back. I know you are. But you might oughtta come sooner than you planned. You an me got things to settle. If you care bout your ant Hattie you best come soon as you git this letter.*

Laura gasped. Her hands shook as she turned the paper over and back. Nothing else. No signature. No other details. Yet she knew who it came from. Curry Porter had managed to get away the night her father died but he'd been hell bent on making Laura suffer.

She thought of the Ashe County sheriff, Blaine Wilson, and her stomach fluttered. He hadn't wanted Laura to get involved again. He'd assured her he wouldn't quit searching till he found her uncle. Yet the man had slipped away right under their noses, even after Laura had shot him. And now he was back, threatening her Aunt Hattie.

CHAPTER 2

Porter's Hollow, NC
Saturday, October 30, 2010

Curry Porter crouched in the center of a damp cave as contorted shadows performed a primitive dance on the walls around him. Orange flames reflected off a set of blue-glass mason jars.

It'd been nearly three weeks since Glen's girl, Laura, had set her eyes on Curry to do him in, and lost her daddy instead. And she thought she'd found out his secrets. She didn't know the half of it. She was his niece—blood kin—but what she'd done prying into his business and setting the sheriff on him made her of no account. No matter how much his momma declared what mattered most was blood.

The hard, withered man rocked on his haunches, his gaze fixed on a single jar. Its contents sparkled in the flickering glow. Sparkling wet. Wet like eyes. The eyes, that's what haunted him. *"Windows of the soul,"* his momma said, but Beulah Porter couldn't help him now. The contents of the jars stared at him, silently accusing. They were all like Delilah with Samson, robbing men of strength, lying and taunting.

His brother Loy's friend, Lottie Edwards, was the first girl he'd ever gone that far with. Been tempted plenty of times. The girls he knew in Porter's Hollow teased him enough, but their daddies would've skinned his hide if he ever touched one of 'em.

He had something that gnawed at his insides though, like a bad itch you couldn't reach or do nothing about, and it hankered to be satisfied.

Course, there were all those girls him and Glen met when they were out hunting for work. But they would just look at each other and giggle, twirling their ponytails around their fingers, and spying on him over their shoulders. Always teasing but never letting him get them alone.

Then came Marybeth. The night he met her, she sat beside him at the movies and went along to the diner after. Marybeth had blonde hair so long it hung down the back of her legs. Her fair skin was smooth and cool as milk. She leaned in close, her half-lidded eyes enticing him. Sparkly purplish blue eyes, like Lobelia bloomin' on the mountain above Porter's Hollow.

Marybeth snuggled up to him all evening long, talking, smiling up at him with those eyes. She let him walk her home. They even wandered off a side road and ended up in a field alone. She sat down with her back against a big rock and patted the spot beside her in the moonlight, and he'd obeyed like a dumb mutt.

When he went to kiss her, she pushed him away at first, but he didn't give up easy. When he was on top of her, she sighed in his ear all sweet and soft till he thought he couldn't take it anymore. Then, she shoved him hard, jumped up and stood over him laughing. Before he could react, she ran off and left him laying there feeling like a fool. It was the last time a girl would get the better of him. The last time one would get the chance to make *him* feel like a halfwit.

Not long afterward, him and his brothers got a job bringing in the tobacco harvest out in Lowgap. While they were there, he got the sense something was changing. He'd been stewing and angry. His insides churned. He felt it in his bones, saw it in his own reflection in the mirror. It burned in his groin.

At the same time, he'd sensed the creature's presence. It'd been following him and his brothers for weeks as they came and went. Some nights he would sit alone in the woods with a jug of 'shine, peering into the darkness, waiting, sensing it out there watching.

On the night he took Lottie Edwards, it finally happened.

Somehow that night, it took over his mind and body. He hadn't really wanted to hurt the girl, but the beast made him do things. Things that gave him power. Things that darkened those bright, slanty blue eyes, and left Lottie Edwards in a trembling heap. Till his brother Glen stepped in and ended it. Curry hadn't actually killed Lottie himself, it was Glen's hand the creature used to bash the girl's skull with a rock.

Curry couldn't explain it. One minute he was filled with a strength and boldness he never had before, and the next he was shaking with fear, and sick... sick to his stomach. 'Course that was before he knew anything about the creature.

In all the confusion that night, him and Glen had forgot about Loy. Their little brother had run off and hid somewhere. Loy wasn't too bright. Dumb as a door nail, truth be told. Guess it scared him awful bad seeing Lottie on the ground all bloody and still. But he came wandering home just before daybreak. They met him in the woods out back of their momma's house and put the fear of God in him so he wouldn't tell nobody what happened.

Curry gave him a special scare, running the flat side of his great granddaddy's old bowie knife along Loy's throat. Didn't take much to scare his kind. *Retard's afraid a everything.*

Afterward they sent Loy inside, and Glen went to be with his young wife, but Curry headed back out into the woods. The woods—and the caves up in the mountain above Porter's Hollow—where he could think. That was the day the beast showed itself outright.

He'd sat in the very same cave he was in now, staring at the firelight flickering on the walls, when the shadows it created began to take shape. A large dark shape, like a wolf on all fours. It grew taller than a man as it stood upright, stretching its tremendous front legs up and out, flexing paws that formed into claw-like hands. Its massive form was covered in coarse greyish-black hair, its thick legs ending in clawed feet, its shoulders wide and heavily muscled.

Then it turned and looked at him, yellow-amber eyes glowing in the firelight.

Curry hadn't moved. He sat watching the creature, his gaze fixed on those eyes. Then it spoke to him. Not in words—*in his soul.* Curry never said a word either, but the beast came full on him this time, filling him near to bursting with power. His chest rose, his shoulders swelled and he raised his neck and flexed. He tilted his head back and let its strength fill him. Never again would he let a woman get the better of him. Never again would a female make him feel powerless.

And none had, until that upstart daughter of Glen's came back to the hollow and ruined everything. She'd even managed to get Loy to help. 'Cause of Laura Allen Evans, Glen was dead. Curry couldn't go back to his own home. Couldn't visit his momma, or help his retarded brother. Didn't even have his rifle.

But he still had his great granddaddy's old bowie knife. The one he always used to... He'd use it on *her* this time.

He stood and stretched then, reaching for the shovel that leaned against the wall. Time to pick a new spot to bury his treasure. He placed the jars in one by one, separating them with soft dirt. When he was done, he tamped the surface and laid a flat rock over top.

Yet this time, he held one jar out separate. He'd have to give up some of his precious treasure. It was what the creature wanted him to do. Curry knew it in his mind and soul, though words had never passed between them, and he'd come to learn he had to obey. There was a tradeoff for all that power and pleasure. He'd found out the hard way once when he'd tried to resist the demon beast.

Ah well, it was too late for him now. He belonged to the creature as surely as both his granddaddy and his great granddaddy.

He stood to study his handiwork, picturing Laura Allen's eyes, and his jaw clenched and his upper lip twitched. He'd had her in his grasp and lost her, but she'd be back. He'd made sure she got a special invitation to visit him here in his new home.

And this time, the beast would make sure she couldn't run off.

CHAPTER 3

West Jefferson, NC
Saturday, October 30, 2010

Blaine Wilson pushed the sliding glass door aside with one hand, and grasped a mug of steaming black coffee in the other as he let Duke out. The dog bounded down the steps and out onto the lawn. The Ashe County Sheriff took a slow sip, steam rising in front of his face in the early morning chill. The sun hadn't yet broken out above the tree line.

Blaine was up at five every day, an old army habit he'd gotten so used to that anything else felt wrong. He'd already done PT—another unshakeable military habit—packed his rucksack in preparation for the day, ate breakfast, showered, and fed Duke.

Billed as a Malamute-Shepherd mix, which turned out to be more of a color and type description, the dog had come from a shelter Blaine found online. They'd said there was no way to know the dog's real breeding, but he was a wolf hybrid. He'd been the runt of a litter found abandoned along the highway. A benevolent passerby brought them in to the shelter.

At eighteen months, Duke was built like a wolf. Large through the shoulders and chest, narrower through the belly and hip, he weighed 120 pounds and stood 29 inches. His thick fur was a mottled mix of black, grey and brown, and he had one amber-brown eye, and one blue-white.

Wolf-hybrids could be aggressive, and sometimes Duke would get his hackles up without warning. He'd growl low and deep in his chest, but the dog had never gone after anyone. Not yet.

Duke was obedient for the most part, though he had an independent spirit, so Blaine spent a lot of time with him, curbing bad habits, and desensitizing him to ordinary stuff. Not every bird or squirrel on a trail required a K-9 full alert. Yet there were still moments Duke would peer off into the distance with the instinctive wariness of his wilder cousins.

Blaine laughed when the dog stood on his hind legs, batting at a late-season flutter of monarchs. "Not such a tough guy after all, are you, boy?" Duke eyed him for a second, then turned his attention back to the butterfly chase. He wasn't living up to his namesake this morning.

Raised on war movies and old westerns, Blaine named the dog after John Wayne, aka "the Duke," his father's favorite cowboy. The canine trotted up the steps to sit at his master's side and Blaine rubbed his head. "Good boy. Come on Malamutt, what do you say we take a hike out in Porter's Hollow today?"

Duke stood to attention at the word 'hike.'

As the two re-entered the cabin, Blaine contemplated the phone on the wall. He pressed his lips together and shook his head. He'd lost track of how many times he passed the thing thinking he should call Laura and see how she was doing. It would be polite—friendly.

Blaine gave Duke fresh water, but thoughts of green eyes and honey brown hair distracted him. Laura was single, close to his age—and beautiful. But every time he picked up the phone to dial her number, his pulse quickened, and he couldn't think of one intelligent thing to say.

He'd been tough on her before she left, but he had to make sure she didn't try to go out again on her own to search for her uncle. The man was vicious, and murderous, and likely insane. Curry had claimed everything he and Glen had done was because of some demonic beast. It reminded Blaine of the stories he'd heard growing up about a creature that roamed Porter's Hollow preying on people who dared wander the mountain at night.

He didn't consider himself a religious man, though if asked he'd have to say he believed in a higher power. In his estimation, life was too intricately balanced, too delicately woven together, too unique and complicated to have happened by sheer accident.

He didn't know much about theology either, but he knew the spirit of a man could be tormented by his decisions. Hell, he had his own demons—but actual possession by another entity, an evil spirit? He'd have to drop by and have a talk with the Reverend Honeywell. If only for Laura's sake. She declared she'd seen something large, like a wolf walking upright, in Curry's trailer the night her father died.

But Blaine had more practical matters to tend to right now. "Got plans this morning, don't we, buddy?"

Duke responded with a *wuff* and shoved his nose into Blaine's palm. The sheriff rubbed the dog between the ears again. "Sometimes I get the feeling you know exactly what I'm thinking. I'll call her soon. Today we've got work to do, see if we can't flush out this uncle of hers."

He grabbed a leash from a set of hooks by the door and a few bottles of water from the fridge. Then he retrieved a travel dish from the dog's supply cupboard, along with a bag of treats, and stuffed it all in Duke's pack.

Grassy Creek was near the Virginia border, about a half hour drive from Blaine's home in West Jefferson. Porter's Hollow lay a short distance outside the tiny unincorporated village, in the mountain behind Hattie Perkins' home. He wanted to go back out there and poke around again. He'd leave the Durango in her driveway, and this time he'd hike the whole damn hollow on foot. There had to be evidence they'd all missed.

His deputies had covered the area around Curry's trailer out near Lansing, but the man's trail died off along the rocky banks of Big Horse Creek, and the police dogs hadn't been able to pick it up again. He must've stayed in the creek far enough to lose the animals, in the icy-cold water. Curry knew these woods and mountains as well as any wild creature. Chances were, he'd eventually find his way back to Porter's Hollow.

The man hadn't disappeared. He was out there, and Blaine hoped Duke might help find him. He'd worked with the dog for months, teaching him to follow a scent trail. The shirt he'd taken from Curry's bedroom should still have enough of the man's smell. He wanted to have his quarry treed and brought down before he contacted Laura. Something he'd seen in her eyes made him want to do it—for her.

Blaine wasn't normally a sentimental man. Life had taught him it was a weakness, and his experience with women taught him to be cautious about caring too deeply. His first and only wife had left when he told her he'd re-enlisted in the army. He'd explained his plan to make a career of it, but that was when she told him she wanted nothing more to do with him. That was 1977.

His father died in '86 and his third enlistment was over in '87. By then he'd given up on the lifelong career in the army idea. Somehow, he'd lost the heart for it, and for love. Now he was just a small-town sheriff with no greater aim than to care for the people he served right here in Ashe County, North Carolina.

Yet, something about Laura Evans brought out his protective side. Mad as he'd gotten at her for putting herself in danger during the search for her father, he couldn't deny an uncommon need to comfort and reassure this woman—and that made him nervous.

CHAPTER 4

Jacobus, PA

Considering all the boxes and the mess still scattered around the room, Laura knew she wouldn't finish this job today. Curry Porter's threat was too real. She picked up the note from the table. *It had to be him.* She'd tried her aunt's number several times, but it kept ringing busy. The trip couldn't wait till Thanksgiving now, she needed to get to Aunt Hattie as soon as possible.

She packed her car and made more phone calls, mind racing, creating terrifying images of the petite, white-haired woman in the clutches of that—thing. If that creature ever got hold of her, Hattie would break like a china doll.

Laura's next visit to North Carolina should have been a pleasure trip. She and her daughter Tara, along with her mother Roberta Maitlin, had plans to spend their first holiday with Aunt Hattie as a family. Her newfound half-brother, the reverend Cecil Thomas Honeywell and his wife Elizabeth would be there along with their two adult children, their spouses, and several grandkids. But instead of the glowing warmth of a family reunion, she was returning with fear clutching at her heart and grasping at her mind with its cold tentacles.

"Blaine Wilson here. Leave me a message and I'll get back to you 'soon as I can." All those years in the army hadn't eliminated the man's accent. He might use a wider vocabulary than most local people, and he didn't drop the g's off the end of words like some, but the sound of his voice still marked him as southern born and bred. The no nonsense way he spoke brought a mental image of the sheriff to mind, and a warm flush to her cheeks.

Laura kept her own response brief. "I need to talk to you. Call me when you get this. It's urgent."

When she didn't get an answer from Blaine, she called the Ashe County Law Enforcement Center. The receptionist answered. "I'm sorry honey, but the sheriff won't be in today. You say this is about Hattie Perkins? Don't you worry none, sweetie, I'll send one a the deputies out to check on her. I'm sure she's just out and about, not hearin' the phone."

Laura hung up, brows drawn, body tense. She knew they'd do their best, but she refused to sit around waiting to hear back.

She called Tara and Robey, but had to leave messages for them also. It seemed no one was answering the phone today. After canceling her Monday appointment with the realtor, Laura took one last glance around the disheveled house and pulled the door shut with a thud.

Her neighbor Lynne was gone, so Laura wrote her a note and slipped it between the front doors. She'd watch over things. It was 12:30 in the afternoon when Laura finally scrambled into her car and made one last call. She actually hoped to get the voicemail for this one, but no luck. Her supervisor answered on the second ring.

"Shelly, it's Laura."

"Yes?" The woman dragged the word out.

"I," Laura drew a deep breath, "I won't be in next week. In fact—I'm not sure when I'll be back." She waited for a reaction but Shelly remained silent. "It's my Aunt Hattie. Something's wrong. I have reason to believe she's in danger."

There was a loud sigh on the other end of the line. "I can't keep scheduling around you."

Laura hesitated before answering. "I'm really sorry, but I have no choice. I have to go."

"Don't they have police in North Carolina?" Shelly paused, then added, "Never mind. It's obvious you've already made your decision. Goodbye, Laura." She hung up without waiting for a reply.

Laura's stomach was in knots as she backed out of the garage, but she couldn't think about job issues right now. She had to get to Aunt Hattie. If she didn't stop, she could make it to Grassy Creek in six and a half hours. Still, Aunt Hattie lived alone in the mountains outside of town, miles from the Ashe County Sheriff's office. What if she got there too late?

She bit her lip at the thought of seeing Blaine Wilson again. He'd given her a stern warning about searching for her uncle, but he also promised to watch out for Hattie Perkins. Surely, he'd understand.

She pictured the man's green eyes and buzz cut hair as he'd towered above her, and her face grew warm. She hadn't been able to get the sheriff out of her head since he'd given her that last little smile and the two-fingered salute when he said goodbye. *Damn, woman. Doug's only been gone a few months, and you've got a lot more to worry about right now than... that!*

Laura drove for more than five hours, but nature finally called. She pulled into a roadside rest stop on I-81 in Radford, Virginia. She used the facilities and bought a bottle of water from the machines.

Then she walked out of the vending shelter and stopped. If humans could get their hackles up, hers were on alert. She surveyed the area, her gaze drawn by a flash of blue in the trees behind the building. Laura stood frozen for eternal seconds. The darkening shadows in the woods seem to whisper. A chill spread through her and she shuddered as she recognized the same feeling that had come with the vision earlier. Her breath grew shallow. She didn't have time to go following ghosts—reality was frightening enough—but then Lottie Edwards appeared beside a pine tree, one small, pale hand against its trunk, her sad eyes imploring her to follow.

The late afternoon sun had already cast the hillside above in deepening shadows, but now the world had faded to a bluish-grey twilight. Lottie turned away and disappeared. Laura's feet crunched the dying leaves as she entered the grove of trees, but she became aware of another sound, a quiet whimper. She spotted the little girl hunched down between a pair of rocks as a dark mist formed around them. Laura opened her mouth to speak but the child stood and walked away, her pale blue dress torn and dirty, her blonde hair full of leaves. She glanced back once, then again. Laura hurried after her, overcome by an urgent need to catch up with the familiar figure.

The heavy mist wet her skin and she could smell the damp, musty earth. Laura came up behind the girl and laid a hand on her shoulder. Except for the absence of any warmth, she felt real. Lottie Edwards turned to face Laura, her eyes full of pain and frustrated silence. The child hung her head. When Lottie looked back up, she crooked one finger, motioning for Laura. Ice cold fear formed a knot in Laura's stomach. Still she followed.

They wandered on and on through the trees. The only familiar sight had been the old Hadley place. Laura counted at least two other cabins off in the distance, deep in the woods, as they walked. At last they came to a familiar rocky cliff.

This time, Lottie reached for Laura's hand, her touch so cold it sent icy chills up Laura's arm. Then the girl led her down a steep trail that skirted the outcrop, where they rounded the hill to stand directly below the rocks. The girl stared transfixed, pointing into the yawning maw of a cave. Laura watched Lottie's face for a moment. *You want me to go in there?* The child kept pointing.

Laura crept into the opening. At first, she couldn't see far ahead, but a flickering glow, like firelight, grew as she advanced. She turned to look back and found Lottie following her at a distance. Guessing the girl couldn't communicate verbally, Laura peered into the child's sad, sentient eyes—eyes that pleaded for understanding.

Rounding a bend in the cave slow and quiet, staying close to the rock wall, Laura had to bend over now, the ceiling getting lower as she went. She peered around the last edge of rock jutting in front of her. There, in a large open room sat a thin, old man. He crouched on his haunches, huddled over several blue mason jars.

Then he picked one up and held it in front of his face as he tapped the glass with a long withered finger and mumbled.

Lottie reached for her then and pulled hard on her sleeve. Laura reacted from instinct and pulled away, stumbling forward.

Curry looked up from his jar and glared at her. Hate burned in his face as he turned toward Laura. His eyes glowed yellow and his face morphed into a twisted evil thing. His fingers got longer and thicker as he set the jar down, and when he lunged for her, the heavy odor of animal musk stung her nose and eyes.

Laura didn't wait to see what he would become. She turned and ran with Lottie just out of reach ahead of her. She focused on the pale blue of the little girl's dress and scrambled as fast as she could, but the beast's hot breath wafted over her back with each snarling puff. The creature that embodied Curry Porter was so close behind her now the smell made her choke.

In the next instant, Laura stumbled on a tree root and nearly fell. She slapped both hands onto a huge maple and caught herself before plunging to the ground. She clung tightly to the trunk, its bark scraping her hands as she gasped for air. Looking up, she realized she was back in the woods above the rest stop. She gawked at her raw skin, the pain somehow comforting. Scanning the area around her, she realized she'd only run a few yards, and mere minutes had passed.

Laura needed to talk to Blaine Wilson. They had to find that cave. Something vile and malicious lurked there, something with which her uncle had made an evil pact.

She checked her watch. She could be at Aunt Hattie's by seven o'clock if she hustled.

The last few miles flew by in a blur with Laura clenching the wheel so hard her scraped hands hurt. Breathing hard, fighting back tears, the memory of the vision looming in her mind, she struggled to hold back the darkness descending on her world. As she turned down Aunt Hattie's lane, she spotted the blue and white flashing lights of a police cruiser, and her heart plummeted.

CHAPTER 5

Grassy Creek, NC

Hattie Perkins bustled around the kitchen most of the morning boxing up old tea towels, cleaning out the refrigerator, and rearranging the contents of drawers and cupboards. *So much to do to get ready for Thanksgiving and I've barely started.*

She stepped into the doorway of the walk-in pantry and looked around. This was going to be a big job. She brushed a tendril of pure white hair out of her face before climbing the small step ladder to reach the higher shelves. Her thin, spotted hands grasped the top rung as she reached for a can of peaches. She hadn't had family in for the holidays in years, hadn't cleaned out the cupboards in almost as many. She didn't have the energy she used to, but by golly, she was determined to do this right. Hattie couldn't stand to entertain without getting the house in order.

Pastor Honeywell and his wife had promised to come over and help on Thanksgiving Day—and no more secrets. Though she'd never been free to tell anyone, Hattie had always known Tom was Laura's half-brother.

"Ah well, all things work together." She sighed. "Even when others mean them for ill." Hattie gave a crooked smile as she realized she was talking to herself again. She'd always had the peculiar habit, especially when working on something or figuring things out. And it wasn't because she'd lived alone too long. She'd always done it, helped clear her mind and put it to the task at hand.

She worked her way around the big pantry wiping jars, replacing shelf paper. She'd been concentrating hard, talking aloud about what she ought to do next when a noise from the sitting room caught her attention. She stopped to listen.

There it was again. Sounded like the floor boards creaking.

Hattie reached out to set a can of green beans back on the shelf but missed. It hit the floor with a *bam*. "Butterfingers," she grumbled as she descended the step ladder to retrieve the container, taking the time to set it in place again before leaving the pantry.

In the sitting room, she frowned when she spotted the open front door. "Must be getting senile." Though she wasn't in the habit of locking her doors during the day, she usually had the good sense to keep them shut in cold weather.

She closed the door and turned to find the large hand-braided sitting room rug flipped up. Must've happened somehow when she dragged the bags of trash and donations outside. It was lucky she hadn't tripped on it. When she righted the edge of the rug, she spotted small clumps of dried mud scattered across it all the way to the La-Z-Boy.

"What in heaven's name?" She inspected the room quizzically, then sighed as she went for the dust pan. She was bent over cleaning up the mess, when someone knocked hard at the door, giving her a bit of a start.

The rapping came again. "Miss Hattie, you in there?" More rapping. Somebody sure was impatient.

"Deputy Richardson," Hattie declared, pulling the door open. "Ain't seen you in a coon's age. What brings you out here on a Saturday mornin'?" Her weathered face broke into a smile, grey eyes sparkling.

Adam Richardson was Sheriff Wilson's youngest deputy, a dark haired, strapping tall fellow with a ready smile and a reassuring voice. "Well, ma'am, I was just checkin' in on you. Got a call from dispatch said your niece was tryin' to call and your phone kept ringin' busy all mornin'. Had her all in a tizzy worryin' about you."

Hattie drew her eyebrows together. "I been awful busy cleanin' but I ain't heard it ring all day." She looked toward the phone table beside the La-Z-Boy recliner. "Well now, that'd be why, I guess." The phone was not in its cradle. "Don't know how I missed that."

Adam stepped past her and reached down between the table and chair, pulling the old-style handset up from the floor by its spiral cord. He placed it back in the cradle. Then he lifted the receiver to his ear, frowning as he hung it up again. "Were you cleanin' in here, Miss Hattie? Maybe you knocked it off dustin' or somethin'."

"No." She thought a moment. "No, I don't believe I was. But I did drag some big bags out to the garage. Must a bumped it somehow." She thought a minute. "Ya know the door was standin' open too, and there was dried mud over here on the rug. I must be gettin' messy in my old age." She studied the phone a few seconds longer, then finally shook her head. "Ah well, never mind. It's all right now."

"Yes ma'am, but your door was unlocked and your phone off the hook." Adam viewed the room quickly as he spoke. "And Miss Laura seemed a might worried. You won't mind if I have a look around, will ya, Miss Hattie?"

She waved a hand. "You had your lunch yet?" The deputy shook his head and Hattie went on. "You come on out to the kitchen when you're done. Got a couple sandwiches in the fridge and a fresh apple pie just waitin' for somebody to stop by. 'Sides, I been at it since before daybreak. Time to set a spell."

"Yes ma'am, I sure will." The deputy's face brightened.

Hattie tried to call Laura to reassure her she was fine, but the phone went to voicemail. She sure hated to talk to those recordings. "Just have to try later."

Adam entered the kitchen a few minutes later. "Well, it looks like everything's a-okay here, Miss Hattie. Give me a minute to call dispatch and let them know the situation is secure, and I'll dive into that lunch you got there."

Hattie had set out a plate with a sandwich heaped full of fresh homemade chicken salad. She slid the still warm pie onto the table and added cream to a steaming mug of coffee, priding herself a bit on remembering how he took it. If Hattie'd served you once, she never forgot your likes and dislikes.

The young deputy sat down across from her and she smiled. "You eat up now," she said as he wolfed down a huge bite of the sandwich and helped himself to a big slice of pie. "Gotta keep up your strength for all that police work. Just be sure to leave a piece for the sheriff. He's out there in the hollow somewhere."

Adam swallowed a mouthful, chasing it with a sip from his mug before he spoke. "Yes, ma'am. I guess he's out searchin' for Curry Porter again. Saw his SUV in the lane."

Hattie nodded. "Said he'd be out till near dark most likely."

Minutes later, the deputy wiped his mouth with a napkin and pushed back from the table. He carried his plate and cup to the sink and turned to Hattie. "I'll stop back later, near the end of my shift. Check on you again, just to be sure."

Hattie followed him to the door. "Don't know that you need to be makin' such a fuss, but you stop in any time, young man. I enjoy the company. You take care now, Deputy."

Adam gave a nod and tipped his hat. "Why don't you lock this door behind me, Miss Hattie? You live out here pretty far by yourself. Best to play it safe."

She smiled and waved through the window as the deputy drove away. "Sure is nice to have such good young people around watching out for things." Even though she'd never had any trouble. Not so much as a chicken stolen from her yard.

She tugged on the curtains to close them when she saw a man ambling along the wooded path beyond her driveway with a hound dog trailing after him. "There's that Porter boy again." Though Loy was a grown man, Hattie had always thought of him as a child, simple minded, but gentle.

Turning away from the window, Hattie shook her head and went back to her work, cleaning and talking to herself about how she'd never once had anything to fear living alone out here in Porter's Hollow.

Head hanging low, Loy Porter scuffed his feet along the dirt road. The autumn sun was finally high enough to warm his bones.

Loy kept an eye on Hattie Perkins' home, watching for Miss Laurie to come back, but he never thought his brother would trouble that nice old lady. Looked like she was okay, but Curry had been there for sure. Rebel smelled him out, and old Reb's nose was nothing to trifle with.

He loved his brother. They were family, blood, even though Curry treated him like he was too dumb to understand or care about things. Truth was, most folks did, except his momma, but he knew plenty.

He knew wrong from right, and he knew it was wrong to hurt people the way his brother had done for years. He was sorry he couldn't do anything to fix Curry, but Miss Laurie was his only niece. She was family too, and a good woman. Kind and caring. Loy didn't think he could bear it if his brother hurt her like he'd done all those others.

CHAPTER 6

Sheriff Wilson's two-way radio crackled and he turned the volume up, waiting.

"Alpha Romeo to Bravo Whiskey? Break. You there, Sheriff? Over."

"Wilson here. Drop the military crap and talk to me." Deputy Richardson was a good kid but he got off on the macho stuff.

"Rog—I mean, Sheriff, we have a situation." He paused, but apparently couldn't resist closing with, "Over."

Blaine shook his head as he answered, "Go ahead."

"It's Miss Perkins. She fell off a ladder and she's refusin' to let me call an ambulance. I see your truck still sittin' here, thought maybe you could come talk some sense into her? Over."

"On my way, but I'm about a mile out. Keep her warm and watch for shock."

"Copy that. Alpha Romeo over and out."

Out would've been sufficient. If the kid was going to use the jargon he ought to get it right. Blaine wasted no time correcting him now. Instead he set out at a ground eating jog with Duke on the leash at his side. He was fit, but in these woods, it could take him ten minutes.

He sprinted the last quarter mile as the fading twilight yielded to darkness. On the open dirt lane, Duke pulled on the lead, trying to dash out ahead. The dog always sensed trouble, and he liked to be the first one on the scene.

Richardson must've called for backup. There were two Ashe County cruisers in the lane, flashing lights reflecting off the barn wall. The men were kneeling on the ground by the tobacco shed with Hattie Perkins between them, chatting with her like they'd come to pay a social call. Thankfully, the woman had a blanket wrapped around her, and she greeted Duke like an old friend, rubbing his head and back. At least she wasn't in any immediate distress.

"Miss Hattie, what are you doing climbing around that old tobacco barn all by yourself?" Blaine gently scolded. "You hurt?" He bent forward to catch his breath and darted a glance at Deputy Richardson.

"No. No, I'm fine, Sheriff," the elderly woman insisted. "Just heard a lot of squallin' out here, so I followed the sound. Figured it was that yella tabby always gettin' itself into a fix. Sound was comin' from up there in the loft, so I started to climb up." Hattie gestured toward the barn and the blanket fell away revealing a thin, weathered arm. "That's when somethin' jumped down on top a me. Guess it must a knocked me for a loop. Don't remember nothin' else till your deputy started hollerin' my name."

The sheriff motioned for Adam Richardson to step aside. "How did you know she needed help? And how'd she get out here? Did you move her?" He stared his deputy hard in the eye.

"Her niece, Miss Evans's been tryin' to call her for hours and it kept ringing busy. But everythin' was fine. Phone was just off the hook. I told her I'd check back on her later because she didn't seem to know how it got that way." The deputy pulled his hat off and scratched his head before going on. "Couldn't find her at first when I come back. So, I checked the barn." Then he gestured to Hattie. "She came out here on her own. Refused to stay put, so I checked her over. She doesn't appear to be injured, but she got this far and just slid to the ground... lightheaded, I guess."

Blaine Wilson sighed hard. "We're going to get you up and into the house, Miss Hattie. Do you think you can walk?"

"Think so, if you don't mind helpin' an old woman up."

Each man took a gentle but firm hold under the elderly woman's arms. The sheriff frowned at the other deputy over his shoulder. "Turn those cruiser lights off." Blaine turned back just in time to see a Toyota Corolla come barreling down the driveway to a gravel crunching halt.

Laura Evans scrambled out of the vehicle and rushed toward them. "What on earth? Why didn't somebody call me?"

CHAPTER 7

Laura discovered her aunt had been so busy she hadn't eaten supper, and she'd been laying out there in the barn for at least an hour when the deputy found her. Still, no matter how hard she tried, she couldn't talk the elderly woman into going to the hospital. It was no wonder by the time she finished helping Hattie clean herself up, her aunt was ready to call it a night.

"I'm sorry dear, I'd love to stay up and talk, but I'm bone weary." She looked at Blaine, "No need to hurry off, Sheriff. You two enjoy yourselves." She gave a weak but sly smile.

Laura stopped in the doorway. "I'll check in on you later, Aunt Hattie." Then she closed the door, with the sheriff at her shoulder. She glanced up at him in the half dark, wanting to speak, but holding her tongue.

In the kitchen, she poured them both a cup of coffee. The sheriff sat down at the table, leaning back in his chair watching her. Laura met his eyes as he reached for his mug. His lips were set in a tight line, his expression difficult to read.

Laura broke the silence. "I don't understand what happened."

Blaine shifted forward in his chair. "I was out in the hollow most of the day searching for signs of Curry. I took Duke along but he kept wanting to take off after rabbit trails. My cell doesn't get any reception out there. It's why I carry the hand-held. Dispatch tried to reach you, though. They said your phone went straight to message."

Laura shook her head. "No, I realize that. I mean, what happened to Aunt Hattie? Your deputy claims she must be getting weaker and just couldn't keep her grip on the ladder. I know she's not that feeble, not yet anyway. If she got lightheaded after she fell, it's understandable."

"I wouldn't worry too much. Hattie Perkins is a tough old girl. She'll probably be alive and kicking long after I'm cold and dead in the grave." He gave a light laugh, but the smile didn't make it to his eyes.

"No, I'm telling you, my uncle's responsible for this." Laura went to her purse and dug out the envelope she'd found in the mail that morning.

She sunk back onto her chair as he read the slip of paper. "This is exactly why I don't want you getting involved. Curry Porter is after *you*. He obviously baited you to get you back here. And it worked."

"I realize that. But I couldn't just ignore this. And when nobody answered my calls, I panicked." Laura huffed and got up from the table to create more space between them. "Then I drive in here and there's police cars and lights flashing. I'm..." she struggled for words. "I'm angry that no one else is taking this as seriously as I do. I'm frustrated that I can't fix this and make her safe. I'm... I'm scared." Laura's shoulders fell. "We have no idea what he may be capable of. No one does. He's crazy—and I believe... he's possessed." There, she finally said it aloud. Laura sat back down watching Blaine's face, sure he was going to think she was loony.

The sheriff gave her a long steady gaze while Duke got up from his resting place on the rug by the sink. The dog laid his muzzle in Laura's lap, blinking up at her. He switched his eyes to his owner and back without lifting his head.

"That dog's a sucker for wounded souls." Blaine gave a sardonic half grin. Then he looked away. "I took him out there in the hollow today because he's gotten pretty good at following a scent trail. He seemed to pick up on something near the old Hadley cabin. We followed it up the mountain a ways, but that's when he got distracted. I circled back and tried again a few times, but I had trouble reining him in after that." The sheriff rubbed his jaw with one hand. "We had to head back before we lost daylight. We weren't far out when Richardson called."

Laura rubbed Duke's head, staring into those vivid, odd colored eyes. She hadn't known Blaine had a dog till tonight. Funny how people revealed themselves in layers. "He's beautiful," she half-whispered, losing herself for a moment in the animal's soft, expressive face.

Blaine cleared his throat. "I've been planning on going to see the preacher."

She looked up, a glimmer of hope lighting her face, but the sheriff raised a hand. "I'm not convinced there's anything... supernatural... going on, but I want to know more about this thing your uncle claims possesses him. Even if it's all in his own head, it's worth knowing more."

Laura bit her bottom lip. Should she tell him about the visions? She thought for a moment before she spoke. "Have you ever been doing something completely ordinary and had a sudden sense of something flash by you? Like something was there in your peripheral vision, but when you turned to look, it slipped away?"

He drew his brows together and lifted a shoulder.

Laura rushed on, "What if, one time, that something that usually disappears doesn't? And you see it? Really see it. And if you keep looking, you find yourself seeing more than you want?"

"What are you trying to say, Laura?"

She looked away before she spoke again. "I think..." she sighed and shook her head. "I've seen Lottie Edwards, and I think she's trying to show me something." Laura looked up at the sheriff then, waiting.

"What do you mean you've *seen* her?"

She dropped her gaze to the dog. "It started when my father called, wanting me to come back here." She paused, her eyes glazing over as she thought back to the first time Lottie Edwards appeared to her. "I kept having these dreams of a little girl with blonde hair in a blue dress. She was always being chased by... something." Laura paused again. "I discovered later on it was Lottie, but when we found out what happened to her, the dreams stopped."

Blaine leaned on his elbow and cupped his mouth with one large work-roughened hand.

"But she's back. Only now it's not a dream. I... I see her. I can touch her. I mean, she's actually there." Laura's eyes flitted from one spot to the next, seeking something to focus on. "It's like a—a vision, I guess. She's there, but she's wrapped in a fog, or haze, or something. Then I follow her and suddenly, we're somewhere else. Somewhere out in the hollow."

Blaine lowered his eyebrows, his gaze fixed on Laura's face. Still he didn't speak.

She swallowed hard. "Twice now she appeared and led me into the hollow past the Hadley cabin. There were a few other old rundown places off in the distance, but we kept going higher up the mountain to a sort of overhang. Then she took me down a path around the cliff and... we ended up in a cave." She stopped to take a long breath. "My uncle was there, but it wasn't really him. I mean... it was him, and yet he changed into something..." She shuddered at the image in her mind and Duke lifted his head, watching her intently. He gave a soft whisper of a whine in his throat.

The furrow between Blaine's eyes deepened. Then he sat back and crossed his arms. "A lot has happened to you lately. You lost your husband, and your daughter left home recently. You found out you have a brother you never knew about. Then you found— and lost—your real father all in the space of about a week. And you've got a deranged uncle out there who wants to hurt you, and maybe your loved ones."

Laura propped her elbow on the table, resting her chin on her fist, but she didn't interrupt. He obviously didn't believe what she'd experienced was real.

"You might be having dreams. That'd be normal. You've got some heavy stuff to deal with." Blaine pushed his chair back and got up from the table. "But right now, I think you need a good night's rest."

Laura stood with him, and Blaine looked down and caught her eye. "Listen, Duke and I can sleep down here in the sitting room tonight. Keep watch so you can sleep. Sound good?"

She bit her lip to stave off tears. He could be patronizing, but she had to admit, she was worried about keeping Aunt Hattie safe. Thinking better of facing their differences on the issue for now, she shrugged, "I guess so."

After bringing him a pillow and blankets, Laura checked in on her aunt. Hattie was breathing normally, her face peaceful. With the sheriff downstairs on the sofa, they should both be able to get a good night's sleep.

Back in the room she'd slept in as a child, Laura noted how little Aunt Hattie had done to change it. The now antique, Waterfall bedroom set still occupied most of the floor space. Her old Sugar Plum doll in the red velveteen coat and hat, with white fur trim, lay propped on the bed pillows. Atop the dresser to the right stood a stack of Little Golden Books.

Aunt Hattie had always been more like a grandmother to her. It felt good to be back again, despite the persistent anxiety about her uncle.

Oh God, I have to find him. She had to know what Lottie was trying to communicate. Curry Porter's story ran deeper than any of them knew. Convinced it had something to do with those caves, Laura determined to find them, even if she had to do it alone.

CHAPTER 8

Sunday, October 31, 2010

The smell of bacon frying and coffee brewing drew Laura into the day. She rolled over to peek at the clock—5:30. Her stomach rumbled. She combed her hair and changed out of her nightshirt, washed up, put on a touch of foundation, and headed downstairs.

In the kitchen, Blaine stirred scrambled eggs in an iron skillet while Hattie turned the bacon. Laura joined them, popping bread in the toaster. "Good morning, Aunt Hattie. Are you feeling better?" Laura reached to hug her aunt as she spoke.

The elderly woman returned Laura's hug. "Oh, I'm fine. Wasn't much of a tumble. Only missed a couple rungs a the ladder. Don't you worry 'bout me none." Hattie's smile faded and lines rippled her forehead as she went on. "I don't mind a bit that you're here, but what made you come back so early? Thought you wasn't comin' till Thanksgivin' Day."

Laura caught the sheriff's eye, biting her lip, wondering if she should tell her aunt about Curry's note. He returned her look with a slight shake of his head.

She understood. It was better not to frighten the woman with her uncle's manic threats. Laura said, "I had a chance to take some extra time off, so I thought I'd surprise you. Never expected to find you injured."

Hattie cocked her head at an angle. "Funny. Hard as I try, I can't really remember much about it, 'cept somethin' swoopin' down..." The elderly woman pursed her lips. Then she added, "Wished I'd a seen what it was."

As Laura set the buttered toast on the table, she watched Blaine help her aunt with her chair, but dropped her gaze when he caught her eye.

Hattie reached for the coffee. "Oh, your momma called. Said she'd be here later today. Can't figure why she'd want to come so early either. Not that I mind. Haven't been blessed with so much company in years."

"I didn't think she'd be coming yet. I mean I called her before I left yesterday, but..." Laura's voice trailed.

"You know you two could move back here if you wanted to. Still plenty a room, and neither one of ya's got anybody at home with ya no more."

"I'm not sure what I'm doing next. I did put the house up for sale. Too much to handle alone." Laura sat back in her chair. "But, much as I love you, and I love it here, I'm not sure I'm ready to make that big of a move."

Laura caught Blaine watching her with a curious expression, as if... *As if what?* She wasn't ready to complete the thought.

"Well, you keep it in mind."

Blaine helped clean up and Hattie made an excuse to leave the room—something about seeing to the laundry. They worked in silence for several minutes before he turned to Laura. "Would you be interested in seeing Duke work a scent trail? He'd probably enjoy showing off."

He let the dog out and stepped back, holding the screen door for Laura. She dropped her eyes, tightness gripping her chest. *For God's sake, breathe.* The toe of her shoe caught the threshold and Laura stumbled. She recovered soon enough but Blaine still lunged after her, wrapping an arm around her middle. *Natural reaction. Any man would do the same.*

This man did a sideways dance step to avoid the closing screen door, taking her with him, his arm still tight around her waist. She lost her balance for real then, all her weight resting between that arm, and his body. Several long seconds went by, neither one speaking. Laura's chest rose and fell in short rhythm. She tipped her head enough to see him out of the corner of her eye, cheeks warm. He watched her without a word, then breathed deep and let go.

Duke chose that moment to come bounding back up the porch steps so Blaine stepped away to greet him. Laura watched the sheriff get down on one knee, rubbing the dog's back and scratching his ears. "Come on, he loves scent games. I'll show you how they work."

Blaine opened the Durango's back hatch. Then he turned toward her, his eyes bright as he continued, "I use stuff like my keys, a glove, anything for him to search for that has a scent he's familiar with. He knows when he finds it, he gets a favorite treat, or toy to play with, but he's progressed beyond that. Now he enjoys doing it just for the fun of it—and the praise."

Laura was intrigued. "I've always been fascinated with animal behavior." She rubbed Duke's scruff and he turned to lick her hand. "I had a Quarter Horse when I was young that I trained to do a few tricks. I still ride whenever I can." She smiled as she smoothed the fur along Duke's back, and he pressed against her leg for more. "We never had a dog though. Doug didn't like animals much, and especially not in the house." She felt her face flush. She hadn't meant to sound critical of her late husband.

Blaine smiled. "Yeah, it's not for everybody. Takes a lot of time and patience to train them right. But when you do," he rubbed the dog between the ears again, "they're the most loyal friend a man— or a woman—could ever have."

The sheriff put what he called a tracking harness on Duke and asked Laura to hold the leash. He held an old glove out for the dog to sniff, then placed it in a plastic bag. Then he walked away across the lane, wound around a few trees and disappeared behind the tobacco shed. A few minutes later, he jogged back.

Blaine flashed a boyish smile at Laura as he took Duke's leash. "You can follow along behind us a few feet." Then he delivered the brisk command. "Find it!"

The dog set his nose to the trail, following Blaine's footpath. When he got to the first tree, he slowed down, circling in the same direction the sheriff had taken. He continued along the trail—nose in the air, nose to the ground, speeding up, slowing down till he turned the corner around the tobacco barn.

About fifty feet beyond the backside of the shed, Duke sniffed at the base of a large bush. He circled it nose down and stopped, then he sat and gave one loud bark.

"Good boy!" The sheriff reeled in the retractable leash, lavishing praise on the dog, and pulled a couple of treats out of his pocket. "When he's focused, he's great, but he's still young. If he loses the scent, he'll get distracted easy."

Blaine handed a few treats to Laura. Getting down on one knee, she praised Duke like he'd done the most wonderful thing in the world a dog could do. He licked her hands and face and laid his paw on her leg.

"I think he's in love." Blaine laughed as he joined them on the ground. He reached up to rub the dog's back. "Can't say I blame him."

Laura's mouth opened on a small rush of breath. Blaine met her gaze but she averted her eyes. The sheriff jumped up and reached for Laura. She studied his outstretched arm for a moment. Then she took his hand, letting him pull her up, but she quickly withdrew, concentrating on brushing the dried grass and dead leaves from her jeans.

Neither one spoke as they headed back to the house shoulder to shoulder, Duke walking quietly beside Blaine. Laura chanced a peek at the sheriff, but he was preoccupied with studying the ground as they walked.

They stopped by the Durango and Blaine put away the dog's gear, turning to her as he closed the hatch. "I guess we better be going. I'm sure your aunt would love to spend more time with you."

Laura shoved her hands in her jean pockets. "I enjoyed watching Duke work. Maybe you two could show me more sometime."

"Yeah, we'll do that." He watched her face as he spoke. "You have my number if you need me. I mean, if that uncle of yours... but, Laura," he paused, and this time the silence was heavy. "Don't go looking for him. Leave that to law enforcement. I want you to know I *am* taking this very seriously, but I don't want to scare your aunt unnecessarily."

Laura returned his gaze this time. Her chest rose, filling her lungs, and her jaw clenched. Why did men think they had to control every situation? "I don't plan to take off on a manhunt alone." She exhaled, biting the words out sharper than she intended. "I just hope he stays away from us."

Blaine unsnapped Duke's leash and the dog jumped into the Durango's passenger seat. The sheriff turned back to her one more time, pressing his mouth into a tight line, studying her face. Then his features relaxed and he gave her that familiar two-fingered salute. "We'll find him, I promise."

When Laura climbed the stairs a few minutes later to grab a shower, she was torn between helplessness and resentment. Knowing Blaine was right only made it worse. With her mind in turmoil, she reached the top step and lifted her head to find the hallway had disappeared. In its place, a mountain path stretched ahead of her. The setting sun flickered through the trees. The cold damp air smelled of wet earth and rotting leaves, like the woods after an autumn rain. As she looked on, clouds obscured the sun and the sky turned grey-white.

She heard the rustling of brush to her left and someone sobbing. Laura's neck resisted as she turned to look, and the smell of animal musk assaulted her senses, making her gasp and cover her mouth. A now familiar, massive wolf-like creature stood over a young woman Laura had never seen. The girl had long dark hair and looked about sixteen. Though Laura was sure she didn't know her, the features of the young woman's face were familiar. Laura had worked with the mentally and physically disabled long enough to recognize the physical traits.

The creature snarled and bared its teeth at the girl. Whimpering, she turned her head toward Laura, mouth open, sad eyes pleading. Laura reached toward the girl, but the distance between them increased. The dizzying effect caused her to sway, and the harder she reached for the child, the farther away she slipped.

Laura stumbled on the top step and went down on both knees in the hallway. She drew in a sharp breath as her eyes darted from floor to ceiling. The blue floral wallpaper and hardwood floor were back where they belonged. She rubbed her face, desperately trying to clear the awful images from her vision.

Laura made her way to her room and sat on the bed. She breathed in, out—in, out—trying to calm her nerves, but her mind raced. The creature had to be her uncle, but that girl wasn't Lottie Edwards.

CHAPTER 9

Laura sat on the porch in a rocking chair, working through the visions in her mind, absently wrapping a finger into the corner of her flannel shirt. Her green eyes stared unseeing across the small, once functioning tobacco farm, replaying the sight of the young girl cowering before the huge beast, her face a mask of fear. The sound of a car engine and gravel crunching announced her mother's arrival and pulled her out of her daze.

Robey stepped out with a frown. "Where's Aunt Hattie?"

Laura took her mother's bag and closed the car door. "She's inside resting. I told her I'd get supper on. It's almost ready. We're having ham and green beans with potatoes, and some of Hattie's home canned corn."

It turned out Hattie was in the kitchen when they came in. Robey went straight to her aunt, and wrapped her in a tender hug. Then Robey stepped back, holding Aunt Hattie at arm's length. "What on earth were you doing clambering around out there in the barn?"

"Now don't you go fussin' over me like everybody else." Hattie shook her head. "You'd think I suddenly aged twenty years. I'm plenty strong enough to do what needs doin' 'round here. I lost my grip on a rung a the ladder and slipped. Ain't nothin' for nobody to go gettin' all heated up about."

Laura set her mother's bag down in the living room. "Supper's almost ready. Mom, why don't you go upstairs and get settled while I set the table?"

Aunt Hattie shook her head and grumbled. "I can still get around this kitchen fine too."

Laura watched the older woman bustle about, putting the food out on the table, tidying up behind herself at the stove. She moved around fine, no limp, no sign of pain in her expression, not a trace of trauma left from her fall. Hattie Perkins was a strong woman for sure. Laura hoped when she reached the other woman's age she would be half as able-bodied.

"Supper's on," Hattie called up the stairs a few minutes later to Robey, then took a seat at the table.

Robey entered and Laura exchanged glances with her mother as they sat down. Robey's eyebrows rose and she mouthed, *"We need to talk."*

The three of them settled into conversation about the old days, Laura's long succession of kittens when she was little, the people and events they remembered. Reminiscing on times when things were so much simpler. They ate with no more talk about the incident of the day before.

They'd just finished cleaning up and were sitting around the table talking when something made a loud crash out on the front porch. Laura and Robey froze.

The next instant, a low menacing growl came from the same direction. Laura stared at the door unable to move as a tingling shock ran through her. Aunt Hattie eased out of her chair and slipped into the pantry without a sound. When she came back seconds later with a shotgun, Laura's mouth dropped open and she stared at the woman in shock.

"Ain't nothin' catchin' me off guard again," Hattie whispered.

Robey stood, hands gripping the edge of the table, and looked wide-eyed from her aunt to her daughter and back again.

Laura went to the elderly woman's side, leaned in close to Hattie's ear and whispered, "Do you mind?" She reached for the 12-gauge. Used to hunting and handling guns, she was confident she'd have a better chance against whatever threat awaited.

The older woman frowned but handed over the weapon and they both crept toward the door as Robey joined them.

The growling sounded again, closer. Laura motioned to Robey to swing the door back quickly on her signal and waved her aunt back to the left, away from the opening. Satisfied Hattie was out of the way, she nodded to her mother. Robey reached for the door and Laura slid the gun bolt forward and back in swift motion.

The first shot rang out a warning. Whatever was out there, she didn't want to wait for it to come bursting in. The shell tore a hole in the screen door and ricocheted off something in the darkness. The growling came again, farther off this time.

Robey rushed to flip off the interior lamp and switch the porch light on, and they all waited, peering into the blackness beyond the weak glow.

Shouldering the damaged screen door, Laura crept outside and scanned the porch. A small pile of glittering blue glass lay shattered at the base of the wall. She bent down, picking up a single shard. She turned it over in her hand, then looked back at the mess. Something wet and sticky gathered under the pieces and... she sucked in her breath and dropped the glass.

Laura rushed into the house and slammed the door, locking it with shaking hands. "Call the sheriff's office," she managed between gulps of air.

Sheriff Wilson arrived about fifteen minutes later, with Deputy Richardson right behind him. Laura sat on a kitchen chair she had placed facing the door. Her hands still cradled the shotgun in her lap when the two men entered the house. Robey and Aunt Hattie kept watching her, since neither one had seen what Laura found out there in the broken glass.

"Laura?" Sheriff Wilson stooped to look her in the eye. "How about you let me take that off your hands?" He was speaking to her like he was talking to a child. She looked up at him and back at the shotgun, then relinquished it to his large, thick hands.

"Sheriff?" Deputy Richardson stuck his head in the doorway. "Somethin' you oughta see."

The women all looked up at once, but Laura jumped and turned to Robey. "Mom, why don't you and Aunt Hattie get some coffee or tea going?" The two of them looked relieved to have something to do. Laura turned to Blaine and he motioned with his head toward the porch. He led the way out, stepping aside as the door closed.

Without a word, his young deputy looked at him and pointed.

"What is it?" the sheriff asked.

"There," the deputy pointed again, "in the glass. That what I think it is?"

The sheriff stooped and shone a flashlight on the debris. "Holy sh... Damn, what happened here?" He looked up at Laura.

She explained most of what they'd experienced, but Laura couldn't bring herself to put the rest into words. "I didn't touch anything but the one piece of glass. The big chunk over there." She pointed. "You can get fingerprints or something, can't you?"

"We'll try. But it's likely been wiped clean. A DNA search on those..." Blaine gestured toward the mess, "should yield something."

The deputy touched a finger to the puddle of liquid and smelled it. "Whew! That's gotta be near a hundred proof."

Sheriff Wilson glared at the man.

"The liquid, it's moonshine, Sheriff. He's preserved the eyes in pure moonshine."

"Oh, God." Laura's stomach lurched and she hung over the porch gagging.

"Jesus." The sheriff stepped to her side and held her hair back. Then he took her arm gently when she straightened. "C'mon, let's get you inside." He looked over his shoulder at the deputy as he turned. "Get some bags and collect this... stuff. And then clean up the porch as best you can."

Back in the house, Laura rinsed her face at the kitchen sink as Blaine stood by, watching her. He handed her a towel, and guided her to a chair, but she couldn't meet his eyes when he crouched down in front of her. She concentrated instead on the ripple of his bicep as he gripped the tall seat back behind Laura's head.

Robey spoke up, "Are you going to tell us what was out there?"

"It was evidence—and it was a threat. Curry Porter's not going to leave Laura, or any of you alone. Not till we catch him."

Laura raked a hand through her hair, her voice barely above a whisper when she answered. "Eyes. In a Mason jar—full of moonshine." She shook her head peering up at Blaine. "Where the..."

Robey gasped and covered her mouth. Aunt Hattie stared wide-eyed.

Blaine rubbed his forehead. "Okay, ladies, it's clear we need to set up a watch. I'll take tonight."

Adam Richardson stepped inside and the sheriff spoke quietly with him. He gave a final nod to the deputy and turned back to the women. "I'm going to set up outside for the night. Probably on the porch most of the time, but I'll likely walk around the area now and then. I want everything locked up. Window latches, doors." He nodded to Hattie. Then he looked down at Laura, who hadn't moved from her chair. His voice softened. "Is there somewhere we can talk, alone?"

She looked up at him, jaw clenched. But when he gave an encouraging smile, she stood and led him into the small back room Hattie referred to as the parlor. He closed the door and turned to Laura, tilting her chin up with his free hand, his eyes searching her face.

She took a deep breath. "I'm okay. Really. It was just a shock. But we have to find him."

He continued to stare into her eyes. "You need to leave that to me."

She turned aside and his hand fell away from her chin. "Do you think they belonged to Lottie Edwards?" Laura directed her attention at Blaine, waiting for an answer.

He concentrated on the thickly carpeted floor for a minute before he spoke. "I don't think so. Not according to your father's written confession. He said Loy hid her under that cabin porch and never told him or Curry about it. Curry wouldn't have known where the body was to—"

Laura gasped. "Then, there are others?"

"We've had a few missing persons cases over the years that were never solved. Every jurisdiction does, especially in mountainous areas." He paused and looked at the ground and back. "Mostly women."

"Oh God." The sight of the horrible creature poised over the helpless child in her vision loomed in Laura's mind. She wanted to tell the sheriff about it, but he wouldn't believe.

Blaine put a hand on her shoulder. "Listen, we don't even know for sure they're human eyes. They could be from a small animal. All the same, I'll assign a watch around the clock and you ladies need to stay close, no going outside at night especially."

Laura shivered and wrapped her arms around herself.

"Look. I'm not trying to scare you. But you need to be strong— and smart about this. He's after you. I'm guessing he blames you for exposing him, and getting Glen killed."

Laura looked up sharply.

"I'm not saying *I* blame you. I'm saying that's probably how he sees it. Any man who could do what he did to a helpless Down Syndrome child and live with himself..." Blaine shook his head, frustration etched in the lines on his face. "His conscience is either seriously warped, or he doesn't have one."

Laura walked the sheriff to the door and stood on the porch with him a moment, unable to resist gawking at the damp spot on the wood in front of her, drawn to the scene of her earlier experience by the sheer horror. She rubbed her upper arms and stared out into the darkness. A stiff breeze blew in, bending the tree branches so they reminded her of large dark ghosts waving their eerie arms. The wind whistled around the garage and the moon cast shadows Laura's vision couldn't pierce. She shuddered. When she glanced at Blaine he was studying her close again.

"I'll be fine." She lifted her chin and set her jaw, determined to keep her wits about her. "I'll sleep on the couch tonight," she said. Irritated at being treated with kid gloves, she added, "With the shotgun."

To her surprise, Blaine didn't argue. He nodded instead. "You're a good shot. Just remember to look first this time 'cause I'll be out here." He gave a crooked grin.

Laura went back inside and got him a blanket and a cup of coffee. He stood to meet her at the door, their hands touching as he took her offerings of comfort. He set the cup on the porch railing, tossed the blanket over the chair, and turned back. He stepped close, brushing her hair back from her shoulder. "Thank you, Laura." He paused, ducking to meet her eyes. "Everything's going to be alright. Just get some sleep."

He asked her to turn off the porch light as they said goodnight, and when he smiled as she closed the door, her stomach gave a leap.

CHAPTER 10

Monday, November 1, 2010

Laura entered the kitchen to find Aunt Hattie busy making pancakes and sausage. She stepped out onto the porch to look for Blaine, but Deputy Richardson greeted her instead. "Mornin', ma'am. The Sheriff had to head home to take care of Duke. Then he's goin' in to the office. Said to tell you he'd be by later this afternoon. Around three. Said you'd probably want to go with him to visit the preacher."

"Thank you, Deputy."

"Call me Adam, ma'am." The young man had sandy blonde hair, his brown eyes twinkled when he spoke, and his cheeks dimpled.

Laura decided it was a smile she couldn't resist, no matter how bad she felt. "Okay, as long as you don't call me ma'am anymore." She held out a hand realizing they'd never been properly introduced.

"Yes, ma'am—I mean, Miss Laura."

"Come have breakfast, Adam." She pushed the battered screen door back for him to grab, and led the way into the kitchen. "You go ahead and get started since you're working."

Aunt Hattie set a plate full of homemade buttermilk pancakes in front of the deputy. "Thank you, Miss Hattie." He made a show of breathing the aroma in deep and letting out a loud sigh. "Mmm, mmm, smells good enough to eat." The deputy slathered the four-pancake stack with butter and poured thick King syrup over it all, then he fork-stabbed about a half dozen links of sausage and dug in. Laura wondered how the man managed to stay so lean.

Robey joined them moments later and the women sat down to eat with the deputy. The conversation was light for most of the meal. No one brought up the events of the night before till the deputy pushed away from the table and carried his plate to the sink.

Robey followed him. "Did somebody send the—um—evidence from yesterday to a lab or something?"

"Yes, ma'am. I took it into the station last night before I went home. Should've gone out first thing this mornin'."

"What are we supposed to do in the meantime? Curry Porter knows his way around these mountains. He could slip in here any time and..."

"That's why we'll be watchin', ma'am. We'll be takin' shifts. Me, the sheriff and a couple other deputies." He stopped and glanced around at all three women. Then he dropped his head. "I better be gettin' back out there. I'll take a walk around the place before I set up on the porch again. But I'll be close. You see or hear anythin', you holler."

With the deputy watching over things outside, Laura and her mother set about helping Aunt Hattie clean closets, reminiscing as they went through boxes of old books, toys, clothes. It turned out to be a healing distraction. The elderly woman had saved everything they'd left behind when Robey had moved herself and Laura out in such a rush. It would be a few day's work to get through it all.

When they finally took a break to share a late lunch with the next deputy who came to replace Adam, it was after one o'clock. Laura excused herself to shower and dress, promising to help more with the cleaning tomorrow. She was going stir crazy. The disturbing visions replayed in her head all day. She couldn't wait to get out of the house a while.

Laura sat in a rocking chair talking with the deputy when Blaine Wilson pulled into the driveway. He climbed the porch steps two at a time and stood looking down at her. A smile played at the corners of his mouth, his lids narrowed and his eyes sparkled as he studied her. Laura smiled in return, but she shifted in her seat and dropped her gaze.

"Adam give you my message?" Blaine finally spoke. He didn't seem to notice the other deputy watching them with a grin.

"He said you'd be coming by for me. Something about going to see Tom."

"I figure it's time to see what we can find out about this creature thing. The preacher once said he'd studied demonology. Seems like the best place to start." He held out his hand for Laura.

She stared into his eyes, still aggravated with him. She wanted to be taken seriously. She'd proved she could handle herself with a gun. She was capable enough to find her way in the wilds—and had survived a violent encounter with Curry the last time she was here. She was perfectly sane in every way, yet he didn't want to believe what she'd told him about the visions. He continued to treat her like a stressed out, distraught woman.

She would have to be patient, give it time, and keep trying to convince him. For now, she chose to say nothing and placed her hand in Blaine's as she rose from her seat. She let him lead her across the driveway. He opened the door to his sheriff's SUV and Laura felt her face warm when he bent across her to pick up his radio. He called in his location and plans for the next couple of hours to the dispatch officer on duty, then leaned across her again to replace the handset. Laura didn't realize she'd been holding her breath until he shut the door and stepped away.

He slid behind the wheel then and glanced at her. She felt the color rise in her cheeks again as he started the SUV. "We'll be going to the church. The preacher said he'd be there working on his Sunday sermon."

The tension eased when he asked about Laura's daughter. She realized this was their first real conversation, one about their everyday lives. She told him about Tara, and losing her first child Barbara to Down's Syndrome, and how she had finally gone to college when Tara started first grade and gotten a Bachelor's Degree in social work.

He said he wasn't surprised to find she'd been working with people with special needs for over twelve years. "You have a deep need to care for people. It's obvious." His eyes traveled over her as they stopped briefly at an intersection.

After several minutes, she asked him what made him want to be sheriff, and he told her about his time in the army.

"I joined in '74, then re-enlisted in '77. Served thirteen years, but when my dad died in '86, they let me come home to take care of things." Blaine got quiet for a minute. "It wasn't the same after that. Dad and I were close and I was his only living son by then. My older brother, George, was killed in 'Nam. It tore Dad up pretty bad and I know he always worried he'd lose me too, and yet I went anyway. I guess I somehow thought I could honor my brother's death by serving in his place. Then one day I realized I was tired of it all. I just wanted to come home. Live a quiet, ordinary small-town life, like Dad, you know? Help the people around me, my people, first hand. Not off half-way across the world blowing..." His voice trailed off, his expression distant.

He was somewhere else and she didn't know if she should speak and break the spell or wait for him to reconnect.

At last he drew a breath and continued, "I came home in '87. Got a job as a deputy, then I was elected sheriff. I just started my second term in office." His face grew solemn, his voice full of loss. "My mother died in '91. That's when I sold everything and built my own place." He paused, giving a sardonic grin. "I'm talking too much."

"No, really. I... I'd like to know more." *Ugh, she sounded like a nervous school girl.*

Blaine glanced at her again and nodded. "Sometime." He put the SUV in park in front of the church. "Hold up."

Laura waited until he came around to her side and opened the door for her. She smiled self-consciously and thanked him.

Reverend Tom Honeywell sat at a large oak desk in front of his computer monitor, his thick fingers laboring over the keyboard when Laura and Blaine stepped in. The preacher got to his feet when he saw her. "Hey little sister, good to see you again." He wrapped her in a bear hug, then stepped back to shake hands with the sheriff. "You too, of course, Sheriff." Tom slapped a hand to Blaine's upper arm. "So, come on in and have a seat." Tom motioned to two chairs in front of his desk.

Laura asked about Tom's wife, Elizabeth. She told him about the incident on the porch the night before, and Aunt Hattie's accident on the ladder. They talked for several minutes before ending in a pregnant pause.

A few seconds later, the preacher broke the silence. "So you said there was something specific you wanted to talk about, Sheriff. Something to do with Curry Porter?"

"You know he blamed what they did to Lottie Edwards on some kind of demon." Tom nodded and Blaine continued. "Laura told me about the night he attacked you, the night Glen got shot. She seems to think Curry looked..." he paused and took a deep breath. "She says he looked different somehow—bigger."

Laura shook her head and interrupted. "No. He looked like a wolf. A huge, dark wolf, standing upright on its hind legs. And his hands were huge and hairy, like claws. He was tearing at Tom." Laura gave a frustrated sigh and looked at her half-brother. "I thought he was going to kill you."

Tom's brow creased. "To be honest, my memory of the attack isn't all that clear. I know I got tore up pretty bad by an old man, and I'm not sure how that was possible. But I didn't really see what hit me."

Laura pressed the issue. "I know you don't believe in the possibility of a man being literally possessed by something that can change him into a creature like that, but I know what I saw that night. I know what I saw in the Hadley cabin when you claimed a bear must've jumped me. And I know what I'm seeing now in..." Laura observed both men quietly for a moment.

Tom gave a puzzled look. "What you're seeing now?"

Laura sat back in her chair, hesitant to go on.

Blaine spoke up. "Your sister tells me she's been having some sort of visions."

The preacher raised an eyebrow and tilted his head.

"She's described areas of the hollow she couldn't possibly know about—and I haven't seen in years."

Laura darted a look at him. He hadn't mentioned before now that he recognized her description.

Blaine gave an apologetic shrug and went on. "We're here to find out what you can tell us about this stuff. Spirits, demons, ghosts... possession. I'm not saying I've bought into all this, but I am starting to wonder. I've always thought people who believe in this stuff will see it, and if you don't, you won't. But Laura says she's never experienced anything like this before." The sheriff stopped and looked from Tom to Laura.

Tom shifted forward in his seat, studying Laura's face. "How long has this been going on?"

"It started with dreams that came on after Dad called me. Lottie kept trying to show me what happened, but I didn't understand. Then a few days ago, I started having some sort of waking visions. And it wasn't just Lottie." She glanced at the sheriff, but went on. "There's been another child at least. It's confusing. I never really believed in this stuff. I still don't know if... if it's real myself. It's hard to accept."

Blaine rubbed a brawny hand over his face and sighed. "There were stories, when we were kids. You've heard them, Tom." He gestured toward the clergyman. "They used to say there was something dark and evil that roamed the woods of Porter's Hollow."

Blaine paused, then looked back at Laura.

"People used to blame some mysterious creature for things that went all the way back to the 1800s. Deaths and disappearances over the years. Always thought of them as just stories. You know, things people tell little kids to keep them from wandering too far from home."

The sheriff directed his gaze at Tom this time. "I looked up some of the cases in the archives earlier today. Almost every time witnesses claimed to have seen the thing, they described it pretty much the same. Something wolf-like that walked on its hind legs, and almost every time someone disappeared mysteriously, the stories would surface again."

Tom sat with his arms crossed, leaning back in his chair as he listened.

Blaine went on, "Could be they all kept building on the same old legend. Like I said, I'm not saying I believe in all this stuff. But with what Laura's experiencing, if I'm going back out there to find Curry, I'd like to have all the information I can on this thing *he* obviously believes in."

Tom sat forward, resting his forearms on the desk. He appeared to stare at a spot on the wall for several seconds. Then he stood, pushed his chair back and went to the bookshelves that lined the right side of the office. He pulled out several thick volumes and dropped them heavily on the desk.

"Demonology 101. Everything you *never* wanted to know about your adversary—the devil—who prowls around Porter's Hollow like a growling wolf, seeking whom he may devour." The preacher grimaced and pushed the stack of books across the desk. "Saint Peter forgive my *ad libitum* paraphrase of scripture, but you get the idea."

Laura opened the top book, the thickest one in the bunch. It was a compiled history of demonology. The faded cover showed a man-like figure standing upright, with a goat's head, long curled horns, and cloven hooves. She flipped through the pages where more and stranger creatures emerged, half-humans, twisting serpents with evil eyes, bearded centaurs, three-headed beasts, and a thin figure with the head of an owl and large wings rising behind it, sitting on the back of a wolf with a sword in its grasp.

Tom sat back in his chair. "Blaine's right, there were always stories of things like this in Porter's Hollow, as far back as I can remember. You probably forgot anything you might have heard about them since you left here so young." He directed his gaze at Laura.

She frowned as she listened. She could recall vague memories about being told not to wander off alone in the hollow. Something to do with boogeymen and wild animals, but nothing specific.

Tom continued to watch Laura as he spoke. "When I found out about our father hiding out, and helped take care of him, he told me the same sort of thing. Though he wouldn't go into detail. Acted like he was afraid to tell me much. Always stopped short of the truth." Tom shook his head and sighed. "I never could decide if I believed him. It's why I took those courses." He nodded toward the books. "It wasn't exactly required curriculum."

Blaine frowned and leaned back, studying the preacher's face. "And was it worth your time?"

"Truth is, I can't say what I learned made me anymore sure either way." Tom stood then and went to the window, staring out toward the woods beyond the church. "But in a nutshell, the Bible, and those books," he turned and pointed at the texts on the desk, "say there are evil angels. Demons that followed Satan in revolt against God, and they were all cast out of Heaven and cursed. Hell is their home, but because their time hasn't come for final judgment yet, they're free to roam the earth. There is research into the idea that they can be introduced, or invited into an area by someone who channels, or conjures them."

Laura studied Tom's face for a moment. Then she looked from him to Blaine and back again, incredulous.

Tom went on. "It's said they can possess human beings, take over their minds and bodies to do whatever the demon wills. Or sometimes they simply influence weak minded humans without actually possessing them. Keep them oppressed, steeped in addictions, troubled in heart, mind, and soul."

Laura sat in rapt attention as he spoke. At the last comment, she thought of their father, hiding out for years, afraid to face his past, controlled by Curry so easily.

"There've been any number of serial killers and other vicious murderers who claimed to have been influenced or possessed by demons. The BTK killer, Dennis Rader, who murdered ten people in the 70s to early 90s, said he had a monster in his head. Sean Sellers, who shot a store clerk and soon afterward both of his own parents in '85, insisted his demon's name was Ezurate. They say even Ted Bundy once claimed to have a dark stranger that hovered near him."

Laura's eyes widened, and she glanced again at Blaine whose face had gone somber.

Tom gestured toward the stack of books. "You're welcome to take those along, but I'll warn you. Some people get so wrapped up in this stuff, it takes over." He stared hard at Laura, his voice ominous. "Before long you're seeing demons in every shadow."

Laura lifted her head and caught her brother's gaze. "I'm not looking to become a Satanist. I just want to know what we're up against." She closed the book cover. "What is this—this—thing I saw, what is it capable of, and why did it choose our family to torment?" Laura sighed deep. "I shot that thing in the neck. I know I did. It stood there holding the wound with a huge clawed hand, then it turned back into my uncle and ran. It hardly fazed him, and then he managed to disappear, evade the search dogs even..."

Blaine shifted in his seat. "Didn't happen to study any psychology in seminary did you, preacher?"

Tom's facial expression lifted, and his mouth puckered a moment before he spoke. "As a matter of fact, I did. That *was* required curriculum."

"Isn't it possible a man can believe in something so deeply he manifests the qualities of such a thing psychologically, even to the point that he begins to manifest them physically?" Blaine argued.

Laura stared at the sheriff, surprised at the depth of his understanding of human nature. Still she realized she shouldn't be, he must have dealt with lots of people with mental and emotional issues in his line of work. Yet, he was obviously having trouble accepting the possibility that Curry's demons could be real.

"You mean, do I think it could all be in his head?" Tom nodded. "I've thought so for years. But since I've never actually seen him when he was—for want of a better term—under the influence. I can't be sure."

Laura looked from one to the other of these two men so calmly discussing the creature as if it was nothing more than a product of her uncle's imagination. She'd heard the thing growl, she'd felt its hot breath and sharp claws before, she'd smelled its stench, and she'd seen it become her uncle after she shot it. She didn't hallucinate the whole incident. If they weren't convinced it was real yet, she didn't know what else she could do to make them believe.

Blaine drew a deep breath and stood up, then he looked down at her. "We'd better get going. I'll be taking a shift at your aunt's again tonight, but we need to run by my place and pick up Duke. I don't like leaving him alone too much."

Laura stood and met Blaine's eyes, biting her lip. Then she averted her gaze and picked up all five volumes Tom had placed on the desk. "I'd like to browse through these at least."

"Better give me one to start on, too." Blaine reached out to carry them for her. "A little light reading," he quipped.

The preacher followed them out to the SUV. "By the way, if I'd known there was anything wrong at Hattie's, I'd have gone to check on her. You can call me anytime, Laura. I am your brother." He opened the car door for her while Blaine put the books in the seat behind her.

"I'm sorry, Tom, I didn't think of it. Have to get used to the idea. But thanks, I'll try to remember in the future." Laura reached up without thinking and hugged him.

His smile widened as he released her. "I'll do a little extra research myself on the hollow, other stuff. There's someone I want to talk to about the stories and rumors. Maybe I can give you a more satisfying answer into what might be going on with Curry.

But don't be too quick to write off his responsibility for the things he's done. That's all I ask, little sister. The devil made me do it is sometimes nothing more than an excuse for a purely evil human being's actions."

"Thank you. I'll keep it in mind." Laura smiled and waved as Blaine backed away.

Tom turned to go back into the church and rubbed his arms against the sudden chill sweeping over him. He hadn't gone more than a few steps when something stopped him in his tracks. Movement on the far side of the cemetery.

Loy Porter stood with both hands on the fence, looking in toward the gravestones, his hound dog, Rebel, at his side.

Tom stood watching, trying to decide if he should go say hello when Loy looked up. The preacher waved but the other man turned away and picked up a lumbering trot toward the woods. The clergyman dropped his head, studying the walk at his feet, a sense of guilt rising to the surface. Though he'd offered once or twice, he never pursued the idea of what he could do to help his special-needs uncle. The man was basically alone in his own small world. His momma was blind, and as far as Tom knew, she'd never even tried to get Loy into any of the social programs available for the disabled.

When the preacher reached the steps to the church he caught the distinct sound of a four-wheeler, one missing its tail pipe, as it revved up and roared off.

CHAPTER 11

When Blaine pulled into his driveway about twenty minutes after he and Laura left the church, it was pushing four o'clock. He needed to get Duke and his gear and get back to Hattie Perkins'. He had to relieve the deputy on duty. Yet, he didn't want to be rude to Laura. "You want to come in?"

He turned to catch her leaning forward, examining the outside of his cabin, her green eyes wide, her mouth slightly open, a soft smile curving her lips. She sat back and nodded, looking up at him. Blaine gave an inward sigh, not accustomed to having his heart drop into his stomach at a woman's look.

He pushed the cabin door open and let Duke out. Then he let her go in ahead of him. He watched as she gazed around the place and couldn't help but feel a swell in his chest at her reaction. He'd built it himself, with a little help from a few friends. Laura stood looking into the vaulted ceiling of the great room as he stepped up beside her.

"Give you the grand tour?" He smiled down at her and she nodded.

When they finished in the kitchen, he turned and said, "I'm going to grab supplies for me and Duke. Can I get you anything? Water, maybe a cup of coffee while you wait?"

"Water's good."

He went to the fridge and brought her back a bottled one. "Make yourself at home. I won't be long."

Laura let Duke back in and sat at the dining room table to examine the cabin more closely. The knotty beams, the rugged but polished wood floors, the colors of the rugs and furniture—hunter green, burgundy, shades of brown, tan, and white throughout the place—all brought the outdoors inside. From where she sat, she faced a set of sliding glass doors overlooking a wide deck, an expanse of lawn below, and the woods beyond. According to Blaine, Ashe Lake lay on the other side of those woods. She couldn't imagine a more serene setting.

It was easy to see what drew him here. For some reason, it made her think of his promise to tell her more about himself. She'd seen the look in his eyes when he talked about his past—it must be anything but serene.

Duke sat down beside her chair and put his nose on her lap, pulling Laura back into the moment. She reached to smooth the fur on his head and neck and he closed his eyes. Mere seconds later, however, the dog jerked up and stood growling. His ears alerted and his hackles rose as the corner of his lip lifted to show a few teeth.

Laura pulled her hand away, but the dog was no longer looking at her. He stood and stretched his nose toward the glass doors and continued to growl, though he didn't leave his spot by her side.

She followed his gaze, looking for what caught his attention. Across the lawn in the edge of the trees she thought she saw...

"Duke," Blaine's voice commanded, "sit."

Blaine reached for Duke's collar. "He won't hurt you, but something's got his back up." He turned to Laura after he attached a leash to the dog. "Stay there."

He started across the room, eyes on the tree line beyond his yard. Duke growled low as they went. Something moved, shifting through the trees. When he slid the door open, he heard a four-wheeler idling slow. It crawled through the woods, its rider looking his way.

Blaine stepped out onto the deck and closed the door behind him. The engine revved. Duke barked loud, pulling hard on his leash. A hound dog bayed in answer and came running out of the weeds and brush, but slid to a stop at the sound of a loud whistle from behind him.

Blaine felt the leash strain against his hold as the two dogs stared each other down at a distance. Duke's nose quivering at the other animal's scent.

Then the hound turned and disappeared back into the woods. The rider took off seconds later but not before his dog bayed again, eliciting a deep echoing bark from Duke.

Blaine shook his head and went back in the cabin. He looked at Laura. Her face was pale and she drew a hesitant breath. "Somebody with a hound dog on a four-wheeler," he said. "Have you seen or heard anything of your uncle Loy since you got back here?"

She glanced up at him before she spoke. "No. I was planning on going to visit him and Granny Beulah soon though."

"Pretty sure it was him. He must've found out you were back." Blaine stopped. Laura looked relieved, but he wasn't sure she should go to Beulah's on her own, not with Curry still out there somewhere. "Listen, do me a favor? Don't plan anything just yet. Not by yourself. I'll take you when I get the chance."

Laura looked away, then stood and faced him with both hands balled into fists. "I think I can manage to visit my own grandmother without an escort."

He sighed. Then he bent down to take Duke's leash off and crossed the room to where she stood. This woman was a confusing mix of fear and bravado. He looked down at her, taking in her honey brown hair and those green eyes daring him to patronize her again. He couldn't resist running his thumb along her hard-set jaw. He decided she wasn't ready for their relationship to go deeper. Just as well, it would only complicate things. He dropped his hand. "We better get moving," he said. "That deputy's going to be put out if we keep him waiting much longer."

CHAPTER 12

"Time to stop for the day. You need to rest," Robey insisted as she stood and stretched her back.

She and Hattie had continued to work most of the afternoon cleaning and sorting things. It was time they took a break. They weren't spring chickens anymore. Hattie was in her mid-eighties and beginning to show her age. At least, Robey thought so, but she hadn't been around the woman for years.

Robey thought she herself had aged well. At sixty-eight, she got around just fine. Barely felt her arthritis most of the time. Heck, she could still run if she had reason to. Granted, she wouldn't win any marathons, but she kept up her health. Rode a bicycle every day at home. Right now she was weary of clearing out closets full of years of clutter. Every album, every piece of clothing, every knick-knack brought up memories she'd buried long ago. It wore on the soul worse than a day's worth of hard work did on the body.

Still, hard as it had been to return to Porter's Hollow after all these years, she was glad now she'd chosen to follow Laura back. Robey was relieved they had overcome most of their differences. She'd recently begun to realize life was short, too short to let old wounds keep them at odds forever. And she realized how much she missed her Aunt Hattie. The woman had raised her like a daughter and she'd accepted Laura from the beginning with an open home, and an open heart.

Tears gathered in her eyes as she watched the elderly woman turn from her work and dust off her dress. Robey swallowed the emotion, rubbing the back of a finger under one eye. "Why don't you go upstairs and lay down a little before supper? It'd do you good."

Hattie frowned at first, pressing her lips in a tight line, but then she sighed deep. "Suppose I am a bit tuckered out."

The older woman headed for the stairs and Robey went to the kitchen to work on supper. Laura and that handsome sheriff would be back soon, and they'd be hungry. The way to a man's heart is through his stomach, they used to say. Maybe it was none of her business, but it'd be nice for Laura to find happiness with a man again. She was too young to live the rest of her life alone, *and that Sheriff sure is a good-looking fella.*

Busy with her thoughts and peeling potatoes, she absent-mindedly pushed a few strands of silver grey hair out of her eyes with a forearm. Then her cell phone rang and her bangs fell back into her face again. Robey blew a little breath up at her forehead with a frown. She never let her hair get this messy at home. Laying down the peeler and wiping her hands, she picked up the phone and answered. "Hello?"

"Grandma, I'm glad I finally got a hold of you. I've been trying since I left work today. You guys must have bad reception down there."

Robey's face relaxed into a smile at the sound of Tara's voice. "I'm sorry, sweetie. It's probably not great. And we've been busy cleaning all day. Might've missed the ring."

"So, how are things going? I couldn't reach Mom."

"Things have been quiet today. Everybody's fine. The sheriff took your Mom over to visit her brother, Tom. They wanted to talk to him about Curry." Robey didn't go into detail. She wasn't sure how much Laura had told Tara and didn't want to create any issues between mother and daughter.

"Okay. Will you tell her I called? Maybe she can give me a buzz tonight or tomorrow?"

"Sure, sweetie. You have a good evening."

"You too, Grandma. Love you."

"Love you too, hon." Robey laid the phone down on the kitchen table and turned back to her work.

Bang, bang, bang!

Adrenaline shot through Robey at the sound and her hand went to her chest. *Good heavens!*

Thinking the deputy needed something, she opened the door, but didn't see anyone. Robey took a step out onto the porch to look around, and in an instant, everything went dark.

CHAPTER 13

Loy stood in the tree line beyond the field that stretched behind Hattie's old tobacco shed. He'd come to see if he could get close enough to check on Miss Laurie. She should be coming back with the sheriff soon.

He had to hide the four-wheeler up in the woods and walk down. He'd tied Rebel to it so the dog wouldn't give them away with his howling.

Miss Laurie sure was hard to get close to these days, what with the sheriff around all the time, and his deputies always at Miss Hattie's.

He was just about to sneak out across the meadow when he spotted somebody coming around the side of the tobacco shed. Looked like the sheriff's deputy. Loy could see the shiny badge on his jacket, but as the man passed the back door of the barn, it opened and somebody walloped the deputy so hard, Loy could hear it all the way out where he stood. It was a far piece away, but he knew his brother well enough. The deputy went down and Curry drew the door shut, disappearing into the shed.

Oh no! No, no, no, no, no, no, no. Loy stood swaying behind a tree, his hands clenched into fists at his chest.

There was nothing he could do. If Cur was there, the beast was too. He had to get away. He couldn't interfere with the creature ever again.

Done that once and ended up worse for wear, and pissing himself. No, Loy didn't want to be near that beast no more, so long as he could help it. Besides, it had too much control over his brother now. He turned then and hurried back to the four-wheeler.

CHAPTER 14

The front door stood open and the deputy was nowhere in sight. Laura jumped out of the SUV as soon as it came to a stop. She took the steps two at a time calling as she went, "Aunt Hattie, Mom? Where are you?"

She rushed into the kitchen as the elderly woman came out of the pantry. "What is it, dear?"

"Are you alright? Where's Mom?"

"I'm fine. I was napping and just came downstairs. Been looking for your momma but I ain't found her yet. Was about to go ask the deputy."

Blaine was right behind Laura. "The deputy's not out front either. Miss Hattie, did you hear anything?"

Hattie's eyes flitted from one to the other, her mouth agape. Laura put both hands on her aunt's shoulders and looked her over. Satisfied the elderly woman was okay, she turned to Blaine.

"Stay in here, both of you." He leveled his gaze at Laura.

She followed him to the door and stood watching. He drew his gun and jogged across the driveway, then he disappeared into the tobacco shed. Moments later he reappeared around the side of the building, helping the deputy toward the house. Laura stumbled out the door running.

The younger man had blood on his hand and he kept reaching up to rub the back of his head. "Let's get him inside," Blaine directed.

Laura offered a shoulder and they helped him up the steps. She went for a cold rag and Aunt Hattie grabbed a first aid kit.

"What happened out there?" the sheriff demanded.

The deputy shook his head. "Not sure. I heard a noise so I went walkin' around the property, checkin' things out." He reached up to touch the knot on the back of his head, and Aunt Hattie swatted his hand away. He flinched and glanced back at the elderly woman. "I went around the back of the barn, and next thing I know somethin' whacked me."

"Did you see my mother out there?" Laura interrupted.

The deputy looked up at her with a grimace. "No, ma'am. She was here in the house when I went out."

"You keep an eye on the ladies." Blaine gave his deputy a hard glare then turned his attention to Laura. "I'll look for Robey." The sheriff started in the house, then he headed back outside. Ten minutes later Blaine returned—alone. "No sign of her, and it's getting dark."

Laura's hand went to her mouth as she sucked in a breath.

"I'm going to have to call for back-up. I'll need to get some men up here with lights. It'll take time." He turned to his deputy. "You should see a doctor. I'll have somebody take you into town."

Aunt Hattie snapped the first aid kit shut and turned to Laura. "We'll get some coffee goin', make sandwiches while the sheriff works." The woman took Laura's face in her withered hands. "Keep busy, say a little prayer. Don't let your mind get to worryin' on things you can't do nothin' about. The sheriff'll do his best to find your momma."

Laura turned from her work when Blaine came back minutes later with his rucksack, and Duke at his side. The dog must've waited patiently in the vehicle until now. She'd nearly forgotten he was there. When he saw her, he responded with a soft whine.

The sheriff unsnapped the leash and Duke ambled over to Laura's side, shoving his nose into her palm, shifting forward till her hand lay on his head. She rubbed his fur and looked up at Blaine. "Can he help?"

The sheriff drew a sigh. "Maybe. Can you get me something of Robey's? Preferably something that hasn't been washed since she wore it last."

Laura left the room and came back with the blouse her mother had worn yesterday. He gazed steadily at her as their hands touched, the silence weighing heavy between them. She hated waiting, and it probably showed in her face.

When Adam and four other deputies arrived, Blaine met them out on the porch. They talked in low voices for several minutes before the sheriff sent the injured man off with one of them. Aunt Hattie set coffee out for the rest as they organized their search.

"We'll attempt to follow her trail with Duke. If Curry Porter has her, he's good at evading search, but maybe he won't have thought about how to cover her scent too." Blaine turned to Deputy Richardson. "You'll stay here and keep watch. If he shows back up here again, remember, you want to try to take him alive."

"Yes, sir."

"I'll meet you outside." The sheriff nodded to the other two and they headed out the door.

He motioned for Laura to follow him into the living room. "I don't know how long we'll be out. Those old caves you described from your—visions? They're way out in the mountains. I only ran across them by accident once on a hunting trip, and that was years ago. We'll try to pick up a scent trail, but if that's where he's hiding out, it'll be tough to find in the dark."

After they left, Laura stood by the door several minutes staring out into the darkness. Her chest constricted, her eyes burning with unshed tears. She rubbed her neck with both hands and sighed before turning back to help Aunt Hattie.

Adam grabbed a cup of coffee and took up his post on the front porch. Satisfied the deputy would watch over them, the older woman agreed to go lay down but Laura couldn't settle. There'd be no sleep for her tonight. She went to the bedroom and retrieved the books Tom loaned her. Then she grabbed her cell phone and a cup of tea, and set herself up at the coffee table beside the sofa.

She sighed deep as she dialed her daughter's number. It was time to tell her about Robey. Tara answered immediately.

"Mom. I thought you'd never call. How are things going there?"

"Hey honey, it's been..." Laura choked on the words. "Things aren't good." She paused, not sure how to break such awful news. "Something's happened. Something terrible."

"What? What is it, Mom?"

"It's your grandma." Laura couldn't stop the hot tears trickling down her face. Tara waited in silence. "She's—disappeared."

"What? But I just talked to her this morning. What do you mean she's disappeared? When? How? What happened?" Tara flooded her with questions.

Laura struggled to control her voice, relaying the events of the day.

"My God, Mom, what are they doing about it? Are they looking for her?"

"The sheriff and several of his men are out now. He has a dog tracking her. They're doing their best." Laura took a deep breath. "But, we think it was Curry. He may have taken her to some old caves out in the hollow. No one quite knows where they are, but... well, I've seen them. In one of those visions."

"Oh, my God." Tara's voice was trembling, and Laura heard her sniffling back tears.

"They'll find her, honey. Don't worry—they'll find her."

They talked a while longer with Tara insisting she'd find someone to substitute teach for her at school and be there as soon as she could. Laura wasn't sure it was a good idea, but Tara and Robey were so close, she couldn't deny her daughter the right to be there if she wanted. Her own mind wouldn't let her rest easy if she hadn't come back for Aunt Hattie's safety, and now she felt responsible for Robey's disappearance.

When Laura hung up she turned to the books on the table and picked up a volume on the theology of demons. She leafed through its pages, until she noticed the steady patter of droplets on the windows. It quickly grew into a heavy shower. *Oh no, why now?* It would be hard enough for the sheriff and his men to find a trail in the dark, now it had to rain?

She paced around the living room, went out to the kitchen for coffee, refilled the deputy's cup, glanced out the window several times as if she'd see them coming back with her mother any second. Finally, she sat back against the sofa pillows, drawing her knees up to prop the book against them. An hour later and several chapters in, her eyes crossed and her head nodded.

Suddenly, she started awake. A young girl in a flannel shirt and blue jeans appeared at the other end of the sofa. A familiar greyish haze shrouded everything. Like always, it was dim and dusky in this vision world.

The girl couldn't have been more than sixteen. The young woman stared through Laura, her brow creased hard, her mouth open, her chest rising and falling fast. Her long hair was tangled and full of leaves and debris, her clothing dirty, her face battered and bruised. As Laura continued to watch, the girl hung her head, her breathing slowed, and she crumpled to the floor.

Laura tried to jump up to go to her, but her body felt wooden. When she got to her feet at last, she stumbled on tree roots. No longer in Aunt Hattie's living room, she struggled to get her bearings. Her breath came in short gasps, she shook her head to clear it, her brain refusing to accept the vision before her eyes, her limbs sluggish.

She pushed through bushes and briars, forcing her body to cooperate. It couldn't be far. They'd only been ten feet apart at the most. Laura broke through the brush into a clearing flooded with moonlight. A substance, dark and wet, congealed into pools in the circle of light and the ground showed signs of a struggle, broken branches, scratched dirt.

Laura dropped to her knees, her right hand coming down in the blackened liquid. She grasped a scrap of clothing laying in the warm wet puddle. Clutching the cloth in her hand, she lifted it to stare at the bloody horror. A second later, she heard an echoing howl somewhere in the distance ahead. But as she peered hard into the darkness, the woods began to recede. Rushing away from her like a funnel storm, a whirling mix of blackness and moonlight sucked away the vision, and Laura found herself at the end of the sofa on her knees.

She drew a sharp breath and struggled to her feet, rubbing her hands on her jeans. She held them in front of her face and gaped at them in the weak glow of the light from above the kitchen stove in the next room. They were clammy, but clean.

She dropped onto the couch and put her face in her hands. *Another victim?* Oh God, how many were there? Laura worked to calm her breathing. Her conscious mind told her there was nothing she could do for them now. They were dead. Still they kept coming to her in visions, one at a time. She wished they'd get it over with—but then again—she feared she'd go insane if there were too many reaching out to her at once.

What did they want from her? Justice? The truth of their existence, of their deaths? Someone to tell their stories? Or were they simply trying to warn her against what awaited in the caves on the mountain if she tried to find her uncle?

Crazy as it sounded, Lottie Edwards reaching out to her made sense. Laura had found out she was born the night Lottie died—not ten miles from where the child was killed by Laura's birth father. Then, when she was only seven years old, she'd found Lottie's bones under an old cabin porch not far from Aunt Hattie's. It made sense, if any of this did, that there might be some connection between her and that child. On a psychic level, it might be considered inevitable. That is, if a person believed in all that paranormal stuff.

This *was* crazy. How did she get to the point she could think of all this as psychic and *not* think she'd lost her mind? What door had she walked through that allowed her to believe she could see into another realm? The physical setting of Porter's Hollow enveloped in perpetual twilight. A Porter's Hollow that only existed in a psychic, paranormal sphere.

CHAPTER 15

Tuesday, November 2, 2010

The old bowie knife slid so sweetly up the tender white belly. Smooth as butter. Reaching inside, he slit the edges of the diaphragm and the guts were exposed. A few more slices here and there and Curry finished dressing and skinning the last animal. Squirrel would have to do for the next few meals.

He pulled a rag from his back pocket and wiped the knife tenderly. Then he dipped it in a bucket of water and repeated the process. Holding it up for inspection, his grey eyes narrowing, he nodded his satisfaction. It needed some sharpening but he couldn't let old Robey die of starvation before he had the chance to draw her daughter in. He'd feed the woman when she woke up, if she behaved. He glanced across the cave at her still form, a momentary flicker of doubt clouding his face. *Too late for me, got to have my dance with the devil one last time.*

He pulled a whet stone from the pack he carried and worked the blade lovingly across it, his mind going back to the image of Laura kneeling beside her dead daddy. *Time to pay.*

At last he stooped to stuff the squirrel entrails into a plastic bag. Then he grabbed his shovel and headed out. When he'd gone what he figured was near a half mile, he dug a hole and buried the leavings. Didn't want to draw other critters into the cave looking for an easy meal. Though there was little chance anything else would dare come close. Not with the scent of the beast so strong about the place.

Curry straightened and stretched. Then he leaned the shovel up against a tree and stood listening. They'd surely be searching again today. He'd spotted them farther down the mountain in the night. They were headed the wrong way, but he wasn't fool enough to think he could hide from them forever. He knew they wouldn't quit till they found Robey, and he didn't rightly care. He only wanted the mother long enough to get to the daughter, make her suffer pain and fear waiting to know if her momma was dead or alive—or worse.

CHAPTER 16

Thump, thump, thump, thump, thump!

Laura jumped at the sound. She hadn't slept a wink since the vision earlier, but she was engrossed in reading.

"Laura."

In her rush to get up she dropped the book from her lap. Her heart raced and she staggered to her feet clumsily.

"Laura!" a low, insistent voice called again.

She headed for the door. It was still dark out but the porch light was on, and Deputy Richardson was supposed to be out there. Moving slow, she eyed the shadow behind the curtained window.

"It's me, Blaine." His voice sounded edgy, and weary.

Laura opened the door to find him leaning with his right hand high against the door jamb. His head hung down, Duke sitting beside his leg, both of them soaked and bedraggled.

Laura stepped back for Blaine to enter, but he shook his head. "Can I get a couple of towels? I don't want to leave a mess all over Hattie's floors."

She hurried upstairs and came back with a small stack of bath towels. He took one and bent down to rub Duke's fur. It took a few to get the dog dried out enough to let him in the house.

"Come on in and let me get you a hot cup of coffee." Laura watched the sheriff as he looked up at her from his position beside Duke. His face was drawn, his eyes dull and red. He hadn't found Robey. That was obvious.

"I could use one. And if it isn't too much trouble maybe a little breakfast," he added, his voice flat. "I'll be back in a minute. Got to get my gear out of the truck."

Duke ambled into the kitchen and laid down on the rug near the sink, looking up at Laura without lifting his head. She rubbed his still damp fur gently.

The sheriff pushed the door open and set his things inside, then took the other towels and dried himself off the best he could. He stooped over and pulled his boots and socks off, tossing them beside the door before entering. Then he rolled his pant legs up at the cuff and rubbed his bare feet on the rug. "Alright if I use the shower? I'll be quiet. Got to get out of this wet stuff."

Laura met him at the door with a steaming mug and he took it in both hands, holding it close to his face. "You know where it is?" she asked.

Blaine took a deep swallow and nodded to her as he picked up his bag and the bundle of towels. Minutes later, he reappeared in the kitchen, so quiet she never heard a floorboard creak. Amazing a man as big as him could move so stealthily.

He stood beside her and breathed deep. "Man, that smells good."

She'd started link sausages cooking, had bread in the toaster waiting to be popped down, and was mixing scrambled eggs. As she poured the eggs into a frying pan, Blaine started the toast. They worked in companionable silence. Though she stole a few glances at him now and then, he focused on the task at hand and didn't look up, his face still solemn.

A few moments later, he set a dish in front of Duke and dropped a few sausages in it along with a piece of buttered toast. Then he gave the dog a bowl of water and patted him on the head. Duke didn't bother to get up. He scarfed down the warm food, lapped water, and laid his head back down.

Blaine refilled his coffee and poured one for Laura. When they sat down to eat, he dug in without a word. She watched him, tugging at the inside of her lip with her teeth, the food on her plate forgotten for the moment.

"We'll talk in a few minutes," he said. "Let me get my stomach settled and get warm." He gave a crooked smile.

Laura gave in and ate.

Finishing first, she got up and filled the sink. The hot soapy water steaming her face created a brief distraction from the torrent of emotions swirling in her mind. When she started to put her dishes in the water, Blaine got up.

"Let me." He reached for the dish rag. "It'll warm me up more."

As he washed and she dried, he finally found his tongue. Relating what happened in their search for Robey, his eyes were sad, face strained. It had started raining shortly after they set out and any trace of a trail washed away quickly. She'd feared as much.

"We pushed on anyway. Duke couldn't pick up the scent. I just kept heading in the general direction where I thought we might find those caves." He stopped and stretched his back.

Laura dropped her gaze, a self-conscious feeling of guilt swept over her. It was her fault they had to be out there, but she reminded herself, she wasn't the villain in this story.

Blaine tilted his head, studying her, his mouth pressed into a hard line. He breathed out before he went on. "Let's sit down." She turned to pull out a kitchen chair, but he took her elbow and guided her to the living room. "In here. On the sofa." He sat down close beside her.

He spotted the book Laura had dropped and picked it up. "A Theology of Demons," he read the title aloud. "Not exactly the best bedtime reading." He dropped the book on the coffee table with a thud. "Look, Laura, maybe it's better if you let me check into this..." he waved a hand, "demon stuff. It can't be good for you to sit here brooding over all this with your mother..."

Laura looked into his green eyes, softened now. By the light? By emotion?

"I have something to show you." Blaine reached into his shirt pocket and pulled out a bracelet of tiny cultured pearls. Simple but elegant.

Laura covered her mouth with one hand and gasped, staring at the bracelet. It hurt to look at it. She didn't want to touch it because that would make it real. She was afraid she'd feel it and know her mother was dead. "No." She shook her head. Then she drew a ragged breath and reached out with one tentative hand.

"It's hers then?" His voice came soft and gentle.

Laura bit her lip hard, nodding as tears spilled down her cheeks. She didn't look up, staring instead at the tiny white beads gleaming in the soft light.

"We found it on the bank by the old pond. Out beyond the Hadley cabin."

Blaine must have cleaned and dried it when he showered earlier. She rolled the minute pearls between her fingers and thumbs, working the bracelet around in a circle like a rosary—picturing Robey's hazel eyes, praying with each bead that her mother was alive and unharmed, stopping to feel each smooth stone, straining to see something—hoping to get a vision. To see with her soul eyes. To feel with her heart. Nothing. No sudden insight into her mother's spirit, no sense of Robey's fate.

"Laura." Blaine's strong but gentle male voice pulled her back from the edge.

She let out a breath. What was she expecting? She was no psychic. Just because she'd had a few weird dreams, and—okay, visions—that didn't mean she'd become some kind of medium, or whatever they were called. Geez, if she wasn't careful, she'd be seeing a psychiatrist.

"Laura," Blaine took both her hands in his, bracelet and all, "I promise we'll go back out, and I'm putting more men on it. Deputy Richardson is rounding them up as we speak."

Laura looked up at him, opening her mouth to take a deep breath. Her chest felt tight. She had trouble filling her lungs. She blew the air out between pursed lips and tried again, but she couldn't get a word out.

Blaine went on, "I'm planning on going in to organize things as soon as another deputy gets here. I'll send the others out to search and try to grab a little shut-eye at the station. But I'll be back out here this afternoon and the men will contact me by radio if they find anything."

Laura finally managed to put into words the horrible possibility her thoughts led to. "It's been hours. Oh, God! What if it's too late? What if he's already..." She couldn't finish the thought.

"No. He took her to get you to react. He won't hurt her, not as long as you're still alive and safe." Blaine attempted to reassure her, but Laura wasn't convinced. He let go of her hands. "Look, I'll leave Duke here with you. If that's okay. He'll watch out for you and it'll give him a quiet place to rest."

She glanced at Duke who raised his head in response to his own name. He blinked at her and raised his muzzle as if to say, "I've got your back." Then he laid his head back down on his paw and continued to flick his gaze between her and Blaine.

"That's fine. He's good company." Laura managed a small smile as she watched the dog.

Blaine gave her instructions on when and what to feed Duke, and a quick crash course in behaviors to watch out for. A new deputy arrived, knocking on the door tentatively. He probably didn't want to wake anyone who wasn't already stirring. Blaine went out on the porch to talk with him.

Laura wondered briefly why Aunt Hattie wasn't up yet. She was such an early bird most of the time, but then she heard the elderly woman making her way down the stairs. The woman's footsteps sounded slow and labored. Laura went to check, worry lines marring her forehead.

The older woman hadn't put her hair up in the usual bun at the nape of her neck. The soft white tresses hung disheveled around her face. Laura remembered sitting on Hattie's bed watching her comb her long hair with a silver brush set. She'd had silky black locks that shimmered with light in those days, and her sun kissed, leathered hands worked patiently through the knots.

Laura's own hair had been a curly, tangled mass of yellowish-brown ringlets then. When Aunt Hattie was finished with her own, she'd pull Laura into her lap. She remembered how soothing it had been to have her aunt gently work through the tangles, every now and then massaging her scalp when a particularly difficult knot made Laura cry out.

"Good morning." She tried, for the elderly woman's sake, to sound cheerful and upbeat.

Aunt Hattie stepped down off the last stair slow and careful, then looked up at Laura. "Don't seem to have as good a balance as I used to all of a sudden." She took the hand Laura offered her and they made their way to the kitchen.

Blaine stooped next to Duke now, giving him quiet encouragement. "You're a good dog. You take care of Miss Laura and Miss Hattie now, you hear me, boy?" Duke gave a woof, and the sheriff ruffled his back. Blaine stood up when the women came in and pulled out a chair for Aunt Hattie.

She sat down and ran her thin hands over her hair, smoothing it away from her face. She looked around at all of them. Then swept her gaze about the kitchen. She gave a little sigh, the puzzled look deepening. "What time is it?"

"It's a little after six, but don't worry. I have breakfast ready to go. You relax. I'll get it for you." Laura pulled in her bottom lip watching the woman. But her aunt just kept staring around the house, her face confused.

A few minutes later, Laura set out a plate of sausage, eggs and toast and poured a cup of coffee. She and Blaine sat down with Hattie and he began to explain the day's plans for her benefit. The elderly woman's expression cleared as they talked and when she finished eating, she took her plate to the sink and washed her own dishes.

The sheriff cleared his throat and glanced at Laura, head tilted to one side, eyes questioning. "The deputy's here. I better get a move on. I need to get things rolling as soon as possible."

Laura nodded. "We'll be fine." She tried to sound braver than she felt for Aunt Hattie's sake.

The older woman smiled at them both. When she spoke again, she was almost back to her normal feisty self. "Yes, we will. We'll be fine, Sheriff. No need to worry. I been livin' out here in these mountains all my life. Seen plenty, and heard plenty more. Ain't nothin' ever scared me out of here. Ain't nobody, not even that old cur of an uncle of Laura's, goin' to scare me now."

Laura and Blaine grinned at each other.

"My goodness," Hattie pulled her hair back with both hands when she caught a glimpse of herself in a nearby wall mirror. "I'm a mess. Why didn't somebody tell me I forgot to pin my hair up?" She fussed at no one in particular and headed upstairs.

When Laura saw Blaine out, the rain had stopped. The new deputy sat on the porch in a thick black jacket and leather gloves, pouring something out of a thermos. A steamy sweet smell wafted on the evening air. Hot chocolate instead of the typical coffee most of the sheriff's men had been drinking. *Mmm, heavenly.* Laura smiled.

An old shagbark hickory tree standing beside the house, stirred briskly in the chill autumn breeze. Its bright yellow leaves, visible in the dim porch light, flurried to the ground with each gust. Laura shivered when she heard an owl hoot from its branches. She wrapped her arms tight around herself. Wasn't there a folktale about the hoot of an owl meaning death was coming for someone? She couldn't help but think of Robey out there in a cold cave fighting for her life.

Laura turned to look for the sheriff. He'd stepped down off the porch and stopped, drawn by the sound of the owl too, no doubt. He shook his head and opened his car door. Then he turned back toward her. With nearly another hour till sunrise, the sky was mostly dark. But in the weak light of a waning moon, she could see Blaine well enough to recognize the two-fingered salute he gave her before climbing into his SUV.

CHAPTER 17

"Oooh... uhhh..." Robey groaned, squeezing her eyelids tight. Then she opened them slowly and blinked hard. The ceiling overhead was a dark mottled grey-black mix, dripping water on her cheek. Its ragged, uneven surface confused her—*a cave*—she was in a cave—*but where?*

Robey lay on her side on the hard floor, her lower back burning with pain. Her head throbbed. Every muscle and joint made themselves known, and her skin was sore. She tried to move, but her whole body clenched. Then she drew a hard breath, sucking deep, trying to think, trying to remember what happened. When she attempted to lift a hand to rub her aching head, she realized they were both bound behind her back, and attached by rope to her ankles. *Hogtied!*

She let her head rest again as a wave of nausea swept through her. Then a few minutes later, Robey managed to get a look at her surroundings by twisting her neck hard to the right, partially lifting her upper body. A fire burned several feet away, its flames creating twisting shapes that flickered across the rock wall like sinister marionette shadows. She was alone, for now at least.

If she could figure out a way to move, she might find a rock edge sharp enough to cut these ropes. Or if worse came to worst, she could burn them in the fire if she could get close enough. Robey tried rolling onto her stomach, wincing at the discomfort in her lower back. But with every attempt, the ropes grew taut, pulling on her aching muscles and joints, tearing into the skin at her wrists and ankles, and each time the pain in her head increased.

"Ahhh!" she cried out. Her ankles chafed with the renewed effort, drawing blood this time. She could stand the pain if she had to, but she started to worry she might get onto her belly and not be able to get back to her side. The thought of being stuck face down, unable to see who or what might come at her seemed a more daunting prospect.

She gave up and laid her head down again on hard stone. Stinging tears gathered in her eyes. Robey was overcome, not with fear or self-pity, but with anger. What the hell did Curry Porter think he was doing messing with her this way, and how the hell could she have walked right into his trap? And where the hell had he dragged her off to? She didn't know of any caves near Aunt Hattie's small farm.

Robey sighed and closed her eyes, overwhelmed with aching pain and nausea. She wasn't the kind of woman even to think in foul language—usually. Not since she'd grown up and got married. She was an example in the community. An upstanding, church-going woman with a home and family. She volunteered at the Goodwill store once a week sorting donations, wrote checks to two of her favorite charities every month, and sang in the choir on first and third Sundays at Faith Christian Church a few miles from her home in Shiloh.

No, Robey was not common, or vulgar—not since she'd rewritten her history in Pennsylvania. Yet, she had been born right here in Grassy Creek to an unwed mother, and never knew her father. She was raised on all the superstitious baloney people here loved to hand down from generation to generation. *Stories invented to keep people ignorant and living in fear.* Her face creased into a hard frown.

To top it all off, she'd been looked down on, called a bastard child and treated like white trash. Even in the '60s, a small country community could be a cruel place to live. Especially if you were low class. Then when her own momma died, Aunt Hattie took her in and things settled for a while. At least until she got pregnant, also out of wedlock, by Glen Porter. Then the gossip flew, and her little girl Laura had borne the brunt of it.

Still, it had taken Glen's involvement in the disappearance of Lottie Edwards, and his eventual refusal to run away with Robey, to push her over the edge. When she left she'd cut all ties—completely. She wanted to leave the past behind, and everything, and everyone in it. She'd done a good job of it for years too. But now here she was, right back where she started, not sure if she would get out alive or die in this hell hole. No wonder she'd resorted to profanity, laying in this cold dank cave waiting for Glen's crazy brother to decide her fate.

Anger welled up inside her and she wanted to scream but her throat was too dry. She sank exhausted to the ground again as another thought came to her. Laura and Aunt Hattie must be worried sick. They had to know by now, and they had to suspect who'd taken her. *Oh God, what if Laura decides to come looking for me by herself?* She was feisty and stubborn enough to try. After all, she'd gone looking for Glen on her own.

Robey cautiously took a deep breath and tried again to think. There must be a way to get to the fire. She raised her head and drew her upper torso down toward her legs despite the pain. Then she pulled her legs, bent at the knees, as far as she could toward her upper body, ignoring the taut ropes. Managing to scoot on her side by pulling up and pushing back with both torso and legs, she inched herself around in a circle till she was facing the fire. Every scooch an agonizing effort, skin scraping rock, flesh and muscle crushed into the floor. The bones in her left knee struck pavement every time, her hip and left arm grating against the hard surface. Blinding white pain darted through her temples.

She stopped to rest, trying to adjust her weight to relieve her hip and arm. After a few minutes, she began again the sideways inchworm effort toward the fire. She'd surely burn herself in the process, but there were likely worse things waiting for her if she was still here when Curry came back. She had to try. It couldn't be more than eight feet away now, but the agony kept her from moving more than five or six inches at a time.

She was within two feet or so and about to turn a circle to see if she could get her back close enough to the fire when she saw it. An old hunting knife lay on the ground on the other side of the fire next to an empty blue mason jar—like the one that had crashed against the porch wall.

She tore her gaze away from the jar, refusing to think about what Curry might have planned. It was the knife she needed to concentrate on. Large and dark, blackened with grime and age, it looked evil. Robey refused to consider what he used it for. At this moment, she needed to figure out how to scoot around the fire and get hold of it. Despite the added distance, it was preferable to getting burned.

She wriggled herself around in a half-circle with her feet toward the flames and started the trip around the fire. By now, her whole body screamed with pain—stiffening joints, burning muscles, stinging skin. She had to stop and rest. Turning her forehead to the cold stone she closed her eyes. With effort, she deliberately slowed her breathing to a gentle rhythm.

Despite the agony wracking her body, Robey fell asleep again. When she opened her eyes, it took a moment to recall where she was. "Oh, God!" she moaned.

The knife still lay by the blue mason jar at least three feet away, but she lifted her head and set her jaw, determined to make it this time. She couldn't get her hands in front of her, so she'd have to manage the knife from the back. When she finally wriggled close enough she had to scoot around to find it with her hands. It was so long and sharp she nicked her fingers several times trying to turn it around.

Robey had found her grip and was working on the rope running to her feet when she heard the clatter of stones. In the next instant, the rope gave and she could stretch her legs out. Repositioning the blade upward, working it in between her hands carefully, she awkwardly attempted to cut the ropes. These were thicker and the knot was hard and tight.

Something clattered again and sweat broke out on Robey's back as she struggled. She'd wound up so close to the fire, the heat burned into her hands. She stopped laboring with the knife for the moment and tried to wriggle away from the flames, accidentally sending the mason jar crashing into rock. That's when she caught a glimpse of a new shadow on the wall. Robey stopped, stiffening as the shape grew larger and closer. Realization swept over her the instant before the knife was yanked from her grasp. A searing pain shot through her left hand.

"Thought you'd outsmart me, did ya?" Curry put his mouth to her ear. He reeked of moonshine and cigarettes, his unshaved beard scratched her skin. He grabbed her arm and twisted her around, and she got her first look at her captor.

His face was sallow and leathered, his skin a mass of scars. His eyes appeared sunken in with dark shadows under them, his body lean, his expression wary. The weeks he'd spent in the mountains alone had left their mark, and though he was the same age as Robey, he looked ten years older. Still, there was plenty of strength in his arms, and he moved with surprising agility.

"Think I'd be dumb enough to leave this beauty layin' around if I was far off?"

He held up the knife, staring at it, firelight glinting from his eyes, his head tilted—*lusting after it!*

In a half-whispered growl, he went on. "Time you an' me got reacquainted. You was my brother's woman after all and it's been years."

He yanked her by the arm into a sitting position, then grabbed a hunk of hair at the back of her head. He jerked her backward against his chest and lay the knife alongside her face. "Not yet," he whispered. Then louder, he repeated, "Not yet. Laurie Allen's gonna come lookin' for her momma. And then..."

He dragged Robey back to the same spot she'd been before she worked so hard to get to the other side of the fire. Pulling her to her feet, he cut the ropes from her hands and duct taped them in front of her this time. The scrapes and bruises stung under the tight, sticky confinement and she swayed as her eyes lost focus. He held onto her as she slid to the floor, fighting to stay awake.

Then he dropped her and left, carrying the knife with him, but he reappeared in a few minutes with a couple of blankets, a bottle of water and something wrapped in foil. He gave her time to drink from the bottle and placed a blanket on the floor, commanding her to sit herself on it with her back to the rock. He unwrapped the foil revealing a chunk of dark, greasy meat he held to her mouth. "Ain't gonna have you dyin' on me—not just yet. Gotta bring your girl out here to visit. Can't have you spoilin' my plans. Ain't no damn woman ever gonna spoil my plans again."

Robey's stomach lurched. She turned her head away.

"Go on, it's just squirrel." He attempted again to feed her the pungent animal flesh but she clamped her lips. "Too proud to eat game anymore, huh?" He sneered and folded the foil package back up, stuffing it in a bag. "Have it your way."

He duct taped her ankles together, draped the other blanket over her body and glanced around the cave. Then, apparently satisfied with his work, he turned and left while Robey slipped away blissfully.

CHAPTER 18

"Your hair is lovely, Aunt Hattie." Laura stood in the bathroom doorway watching the elderly woman make a fuss. "Any way you wear it, it's beautiful." She stepped up behind her aunt and took a familiar silver brush from the aging hands. It couldn't be the same one, of course, but she smiled at the thought. "Let me." She spoke gently. The woman's hair so soft, and snowy white, Laura marveled at the contrast between it and her weathered skin. Hattie closed her eyes and sighed as Laura drew the brush across her scalp. "You used to do this for me when I was little." Speaking softly still, she watched her aunt's reflection in the mirror.

"Mmm hmm, I remember." Hattie raised her chin slightly, drifting off into the past without opening her eyes. "You had such a curly mop."

In the silence that followed, a childish ache filled Laura's chest.

"Your momma didn't have the patience to deal with it." Her aunt gave a small laugh. "She'd get so flustered when you cried."

Laura shaped the wispy hair into a bun and fastened it in place with hair pins. "There, that'll do it."

Hattie opened her eyes and smiled at Laura in the mirror. "Thank you, dear. Now let's see if we can get that pantry closet done this morning."

The two women finished replacing shelf paper and reorganizing cans, jars and boxes. Then the elderly woman decided she wanted to go upstairs and work on the hall closet next. Laura, however, had been working on a plan of her own. She knew Blaine wouldn't approve, but she'd already warned him she needed answers.

"If you don't mind, I think I'll go visit my grandmother. There are some things I've been wanting to ask her, and I'd like to see Loy again. He was pretty upset over things last time I saw him. I'd like to see how he's doing."

Hattie turned to her, eyebrows drawn, mouth pursed. "He was here a couple a days ago. Saw him walkin' out the road toward the hollow with that hound at his heels." She shook her head. "Thought maybe he was checkin' to see if you'd come back yet."

Laura turned to study the older woman's face. "Hmm," she sighed. "Well, maybe it'll be good for him to see I'm alright."

"I suppose." Hattie's frown deepened. "Just don't be gone long. The sheriff'll be worried if you ain't here when he comes."

Laura kissed her aunt on the cheek. "I won't. I'm going to give my daughter a quick call first."

She dialed Tara, but the girl's phone went right to voicemail. She was probably in class. Laura left a message. She tried to sound hopeful and strong, but inside she trembled at the thought of how much time had passed since Robey went missing. She gave Tara Aunt Hattie's phone number and address and said goodbye.

Before heading out, she dialed her boss. "Hello, Shelly? It's Laura. I wanted to touch base with you to let you know what's going on."

"I'm listening."

Laura breathed deep and dove in. "My aunt got injured and she's not doing well. But the worst of it all," Laura's voice caught in her throat, "it's my mother. She's been kidnapped by the uncle I told you about. They can't find her, at least they haven't yet, and I can't leave till all this is—settled."

Shelly sighed. "We hired two new staff members. One has a Bachelor's in Child Psychology. We've been short of trained, educated people. I'm not entirely insensitive to your situation, but we need you back here as soon as possible."

"I know, I know, and I'm really sorry, but you have to understand the position I'm in. I promise to get back to you as soon as I can. I just don't know what else I can do."

Another weighted sigh. "Well, you do whatever you have to, but I can't promise to hold your position if we get to the point we can't manage. Really, Laura, I hope your mother's okay. But I can't help thinking... I just hope you don't end up throwing away your career."

"I'll do my best, but I doubt I'll be back till after the Thanksgiving holiday at least. I'm sorry, Shelly. Really I am." Laura hung up the phone with an inner sigh.

She decided not to mention she was thinking about relocating to North Carolina permanently. She had barely admitted it to herself, but she'd been considering a career change along with selling her home in Pennsylvania already, and things kept pointing her this direction. Laura glanced around her aunt's house, picturing herself living in this setting, and it felt right. She tucked her phone in her purse and headed out the door, her mind already on the upcoming visit with her grandmother.

"Miss Evans." The deputy on the porch straightened in his seat as he greeted her. "You goin' somewhere?"

"Just out for a little while. I'll be back by the time the sheriff gets here." She smiled at the man. "Aunt Hattie has my cell number if anyone needs me." She turned away from the deputy and marched down the steps and straight for her car.

"Uh—yes, ma'am." He fumbled for a reply but Laura didn't look back.

CHAPTER 19

Laura pulled up to the Porter's two-story clapboard, sadly in need of a good white-washing, just after 10:30 a.m. She reached for the door handle and spotted Loy in front of the shed to the right. He was bent over the four-wheeler, a tool box on the ground beside him. The hound dog at his shoulder bobbed its nose, sniffing the man's face every few seconds. When Laura shut the car door, both heads turned toward her, but neither one moved.

She climbed the porch stairs, banged hard on the front door and waited, remembering her grandmother was both slow moving and hard of hearing. Though the ninety-some-year-old woman knew her own house well, glaucoma had claimed her sight long ago. Laura turned to look for her uncle again, but he was gone. She shook her head when she heard the hound bark from inside the house as the door handle rattled.

Beulah's tiny figure filled the narrow opening. No more than five foot tall in her younger days, her head bent forward with age making her shorter still. The elderly woman's chin nearly rested on her chest and though she couldn't see, she strained to lift her milky blank eyes as if trying to stare right through you. When Laura looked directly into those eyes she couldn't hold back a shiver.

"Hello, Granny Beulah. It's Laura, Laura Allen, Glen's daughter. Do you remember me?"

"Well, guess I do. Ain't been that long since you was here last."

"I'm sorry. Yes, you're right." Laura gave a self-conscious laugh. "Would it be alright if I come in for a while?"

"Guess you may as well, since you's here. You can help me with this can a peaches." She thrust the offending thing out into the air, the handheld can-opener still caught in the top. The elderly woman's small hands and short thick fingers were knotted with arthritis. No wonder she passed the task of manual can-opening off to the handiest person.

Following her grandmother into the kitchen, Laura finished opening the peaches and poured them into a bowl.

"Have yerself some if ya want." Beulah tended to speak in short sharp words and sentences that somehow had a way of sounding like you were getting a well-deserved scolding.

"Oh, no. I'm not hungry, but thank you. I appreciate the offer." Laura sat twirling a salt shaker in circles when her attention was drawn to the wallpaper.

A 1950's style, the busy arrangement of color blocks contained pictures of tea pots, cruet sets, pitchers, glasses, and vases. All of them in repeated patterns of pale blue, deep pink, and mustard yellow on a background of two-toned grey colored wheat shocks. The fading paper hung in little strips here and there where it peeled away from the wall, exposing yellowed splotches of plaster beneath. Laura made a mental list of the patterns and designs, wondering what the younger Beulah who had chosen it must have been like. Were they her favorite colors? Did she like pretty tea pots and flowers?

"You come alone?" The sound of Beulah's voice startled Laura.

"I—yes," she stammered. "Aunt Hattie's working on cleaning out closets. I'm sorry, I should have called."

"No need. Don't usually hear the thing, 'less I'm in the room with it. Cur always handled the phone calls." Coming from Beulah, it sounded like an accusation.

This was not going well.

"You come here lookin' for 'im?"

Not well at all.

At that moment, Loy stepped around the door frame into the kitchen and stopped. His head hung down, obscuring his face in shadow.

Beulah turned in his direction though he'd barely made a sound. Her nostrils flared and her forehead wrinkled. "You come on in here and say hello to Miss Laurie," Beulah commanded her grown son like a child.

"Good morning, Loy," Laura greeted him with a warm smile.

He nodded in return and to her surprise took a seat across from her, next to his momma. He stared down at the table, his balding pate shining in the dim light, pale bony hands clasped and resting on the table's edge.

"Got no idea where Cur is." Beulah ignored her disabled son and directed the conversation at Laura again. "Ain't seen 'im. Ain't heared from 'im. My guess, he's took to the woods and won't never *be* seen, nor heared from agin."

"I'm sorry. I didn't mean to bring back bad memories." Laura bit her lip, glancing from mother to son. Loy peeked up at her without lifting his head. "I was hoping maybe you'd show me those family albums again." Laura attempted to break the ice growing thick over the conversation.

Her grandmother pursed her lips. "Guess you got the right to see your family." She turned to her son. "Get me them picture books out a the hutch."

Laura switched chairs, pulling one up beside Beulah as Loy opened a volume, pushing it in front of his mother. Here and there, faded color pictures popped out of their photo corners, some of which were missing. The tiny yellowed labels that survived time revealed names and dates. She described what she saw and her grandmother explained each one.

Loy watched, his gaze intent on the pages, changing expressions flitted across his features. Wide eyes, gentle smiles, scrunched up faces, until Laura began to describe a picture of a young man in a white t-shirt and blue jeans with a dark mop of hair hanging over his forehead. The figure leaned against an old black car. She couldn't read the car's insignia, and had no idea of the make or model.

Loy's eyebrows drew into a frown, his eyes looked pained. "Ford."

Beulah said, "That'd be my Curry. Be about sixteen in that one, I guess. My brother came to visit. Let Cur drive that thing once. Should a never done it. Got such a hankerin' for a vehicle a his own, he near pined away over it. Was years till he could afford one."

Loy pulled the album aside and opened another. Baby pictures, relatives from near and far, wedding photos collected over the years mingled with baptismal certificates, aged greeting cards, and a few well-worn letters tucked between the pages.

Tears gathered in her uncle's eyes as they flipped through the volume. Face drawn, he turned page after page, his mother describing the people and places, till at last he pushed back from the table. Seconds later he got up and left the house.

Beulah shook her head. "Keep goin'. Tell me what you see."

Laura chose another album. This one black with thin gold trim. The binding was loose and pages lay detached, the paper brittle, the pictures in black and white or sepia tone. Her grandmother identified several photos. Then Laura came across one of a man with heavy eyebrows, a thick beard and wildly unkempt dark hair mottled with grey. His arms across his chest in an awkward pose, he held a long hunting knife clutched in his right hand like a trophy. She flipped it over. Printed on the back, badly faded but legible, she read, "J.D. 1883."

Beulah's head came up and she went silent. Laura watched her face go pale. The elderly woman set her blind gaze in a distant past and didn't move for several long minutes. When she did it was to grip her hands together in her lap, working one thin fist in the other, rocking her upper body.

Laura wished she could see what the elderly woman was thinking, like a movie projected on a wall through another person's eyes. "Granny, are you alright?"

Beulah stopped moving, her sightless vision appeared to drop to the table. "That there's your great..." she paused a moment, then dipped her head as she finished, "...great, grandfather, James Delaney Porter."

Though she would never be able to see the images again, Beulah reached for the photo, taking it in both hands, worrying the edges between her thumbs and fingers. Then she thrust the picture back. "You want that?" The question surprised Laura. "You take it. More blood related to you than me. 'Sides, I don't want it around no more." She pressed her lips tight.

Laura hesitated. "Thank you." She couldn't let the conversation end there. She had to press on, she needed to know more. "Granny, could you—would you mind telling me more about him?"

The woman raised her head to Laura, the tension in her features still evident. At last she nodded her head once as if to give grudging acknowledgment of the request. "The holler's named for 'im. Came here just after the civil war. Went and married Sue Ellen Price 'fore anybody knew 'bout 'im."

"What do you mean?"

"Word traveled slow in them days, but it traveled, sooner or later. James Porter looked white enough. 'Turnt out he was the bastard, half-breed son of a slave girl from Georgia."

Laura studied the picture. An aged black and white, poor quality, faded with time and creased where it had been folded often, but she'd taken the man for Caucasian.

"He built a cabin up in the mountain." Beulah gestured with one hand. "People used to say there was somethin' wrong 'bout that place. Say they'd hear strange noises up there. Bones hangin' in the trees all over the woods. Things nobody could explain." She shrugged her shoulders and stared off into the distant past again, not moving for several seconds.

Laura studied the photo. The man's eyes—that's what bothered her she decided. That and the way he held the long-bladed knife.

"Course that was way 'fore my time. But you can still hear strange sounds if you go up there. 'Specially at night." Beulah drew her sweater tight with hands thin, knotty and spotted with age. "Some say that man brought the devil outta Georgia with 'im."

Laura stared at the photo again. She was a direct descendant of this man. If what her grandmother said was true, maybe her visions were some latent inherited ability to communicate with— what? Spirits, demons? Did the possibility exist that she could help find her mother through means other than the sheriff and his men had at their disposal? Or worse yet, was she vulnerable to the supernatural because of this man?

Loy shuffled back into the kitchen with Rebel at his side, his eyes on his mother's face, his expression wary.

"You feed that hound yet?" Beulah's chin came up and she tilted her head.

"Yes'm."

"You clean these picture books up then. Put 'em back in the hutch." The elderly woman didn't waste words. She rose from her seat, pushing back her chair with one hand, holding on to the table with the other, her movements stiff and slow. "Time to nap." Beulah turned her blank gaze on Laura. Her cue to leave.

"Yes, I should be going." She stood and tucked the photo into her purse. "Thank you for having me. I hope I didn't tire you out too much." On impulse, Laura hugged her grandmother tight.

To her surprise, the elderly woman responded, placing both frail hands on Laura's waist as she replied. "You can come agin. I'm always here. Loy, you see Miss Laurie out now."

He obeyed, opening the door for her and following her out to the car. "Be c-c-careful, Miss L-Laurie." He spoke into the dirt at his feet. Then he raised his eyes to meet hers. "He don'—he don' like you much."

Laura thought a moment before she spoke. How much could she expect him to know or understand? He was a kind, but simple man. "Did you know Robey's... missing?" Her voice caught on the word and her eyes stung with unshed tears.

Her uncle looked away. "I know'd it—I know'd there'd be t-trouble." His voice near a whisper as he responded.

Laura wiped the corner of one eye with the back of her hand. "She disappeared yesterday." She watched Loy glance up the mountain into the woods and shove his hands deep into his pockets. "Do you have any idea where he might have taken her?"

"C-caves," he mumbled and sniffed. "D-damn caves."

CHAPTER 20

The Reverend Cecil Thomas Honeywell leaned back in his desk chair and rubbed his face with both hands. Research on demon possession drained him, gave him a headache even, but he'd promised Laura he'd dig into it further. Yet, the deeper he went and the more he learned, the more heavily it weighed on him. In the last half hour or so, the air in the room had become dense—not warm—but thick somehow. He blew out a long breath and tried again to fill his lungs with fresher air.

He had studied demonology in seminary, not because it appealed to him, but because his father Glen Porter had claimed to be under its influence as well as his Uncle Curry. Back then, Tom harbored the hope he could return to the hollow, find his father and exorcise the demons. He hadn't even been successful locating Glen until the dying man had taken it upon himself to contact Laura.

In the interim years, Tom had put the studies out of his mind. He'd always found them disturbing. He'd shelved the books and ignored them, forgetting most of it until Laura's visit. Now he sat here at his computer clicking through page after page of information on the topic. He stretched his neck and stared at the ceiling.

Tom found the abundance of sites on demons, and the theology behind them disturbing. His internet search revealed an assortment of evil beings. Some could transform into animals, some preferred to masquerade as people's dead loved ones. Some of them chose to inhabit certain structures or geographical land areas, some were drawn by cursed objects, some by certain activities or sins, and still others to certain family lines. Popular literature claimed there were different types—the succubus, the incubus, the poltergeist, imps, jikininki, goblins, gorgons, jinns.

Tom's seminary training classified all demons as devils, fallen angels who followed Satan in his revolt against God, evil spirits who tormented human beings in any number of ways. Still, despite being an ordained minister, he was no expert on the topic.

To top it off, one of the beings he'd discovered in his internet search, known simply as a ghoul, sounded an awful lot like his uncle's creature. This thing was no Halloween ghost story either. A ghoul was said to be a creature that took animal or human form and ate the dead, or vulnerable people, like children. *Or maybe the mentally disabled?* The creature supposedly lured them into following it somewhere alone, then attacked and fed on them. The beast currently looking out from his computer screen was a wolf that had red eyes with yellow centers. The preacher's 220-pound, 6-foot, 3-inch frame shuddered.

He clicked out of the screen and shut his computer down, recalling what he'd told Laura about getting too involved in this stuff. He needed fresh air. The Ashe County Public Library was open and it would give him an excuse to get out of the office.

The elderly librarian, Mary Higgins, would be there on a Tuesday. She volunteered her time, and she was full of information the books couldn't provide. The woman was ninety-two and she'd lived in Ashe County all her life. Spry for her age, Miss Mary knew more about this area's history and its people than any computer archive. It was her favorite subject, and she was his favorite parishioner. He might have to spend a couple of hours with her once she got started, but if there were stories of strange happenings to be told, she'd have the low down.

Besides, with Robey missing, and Curry still on the loose, his time might be better spent learning more about the hollow and its inhabitants over the years than figuring out what sort of demon his uncle consorted with. Or thought he did. He'd always known Curry Porter wasn't normal... *but demon possession?* An awfully convenient excuse for being just plain evil.

He found Mary by herself behind the main counter sorting through returns. *No place slower than the Ashe County Library on a Tuesday morning.*

"Hello there, Miss Mary." Tom couldn't hold back a smile at the sight of the gentle woman, her grey head bent over a stack of books, spectacles balanced midway down the bridge of her thin nose.

"Pastor Honeywell." The elderly woman's face brightened. "What brings you in here? You come lookin' for information for a sermon?"

"No ma'am, I came to see you."

"Well now, that's right nice of you, but you can visit me at home anytime, you know?"

"Yes, ma'am." Tom paused to gather his thoughts. "Truth is I *was* looking for some information, just not the kind you can find in books, at least not any books I know of."

Mary pulled her glasses off and dropped them to hang from the brightly beaded chain around her neck. She laid the book stamp down and folded her thin arms in front of her waist. "You're lookin' mighty serious, preacher. What is it you want to know?"

"Your shift here's about over, isn't it? I was hoping you'd join me over at the diner for coffee, if you don't mind? I can take you home then."

She looked at her watch and nodded. "I pretty much leave when I'm ready. The other girls are in back. I'll go get my coat and let 'em know I won't need a ride."

At Rosie's Diner, Tom ordered a full breakfast with his coffee though it was nearly eleven, mostly to encourage Mary to eat something too.

"So, what's so important it brought you out to see an old woman like me on a Tuesday mornin', preacher?"

"I won't beat around the bush, Miss Mary. I'm sure you heard about what happened to Glen and Curry Porter." Tom watched the elderly woman's face as he spoke. "By the way, did you know that Glen was my father?"

She nodded. "I sorta suspected as much. Wouldn't a thought a man could stay hid as long as your daddy did. Terrible thing him gettin' shot like that. Dyin' in his own daughter's arms too." She shook her head. "Porters never did have much luck in life. Been that way ever since James Delaney come to the mountain above that hollow." She stared out the window, eyes distant.

"Delaney? You mean James Porter?"

"Mmm hmm. He come here back in the late 1860s. Took the name Porter so he didn't have to call himself by his master's name no more. That Delaney was a slave owner in Georgia—and James' father if the stories were true—but James wasn't black, mind you. They say he had skin near as white as you and me."

Tom leaned his elbows on the table, frowning hard.

"Trouble came when he tried to pass himself off as white, and folks found out about it. By then he'd already married a white woman." Mary stopped then, looking around the restaurant as if checking whether anyone overheard. "Not a pleasant thing to tell, I expect, but the truth is less often pretty than it is pitiful." She paused and took a sip of her coffee. "They had children, several of 'em, though most didn't live. But there was a set of twins that did. That'd be your great granddaddy Carl and his sister Ruby. I guess you've heard of her."

Tom nodded. "Hmm, I've heard the stories about Rube and the old Hadley cabin up in the mountain, but I never made the connection to the Porter family." He frowned and thought hard for several minutes. "Then she was my great aunt?"

"Sure enough. And James was your great, great grandfather." Their food came and Mary ate daintily, speaking between bites. "My granny used to tell me all kinds of stories about the mountain and the hollow when I was young. She didn't want people to forget 'em. Everything from what plants could be used for what ailments—or other things—to who married who, and who died when and how."

The elderly woman concentrated on her food for several minutes.

Tom thought she'd forgotten their conversation until she spoke in a hushed voice. "James Porter brought black magic to the hollow. Been a curs-ed place ever since."

"What do you mean exactly?"

"I know it sounds crazy. Like somethin' out of a novel by that Stephen King fella. Got a bunch of 'em in the library. But James' momma was a root doctor, a hoodoo witch from Africa. Taught him everything she knew."

Tom looked up from his food, one eyebrow raised.

"They say he consorted with demons up there on the mountain. He supposedly conjured them up to get back at the people who treated him bad. Called him a bastard. Refused to do any trade with him or his family, but that wasn't the worst of it. They say he died fightin' the devil himself. Found the man behind his own cabin, battered, cut up, torn near to shreds, an old bowie knife clutched tight in his hand. So the story goes, anyway."

Tom forgot his food and reached into his pocket for a small notebook. "I don't remember hearing most of this. Would you mind if I take notes?"

"Don't see how anybody's ever goin' to care about some old mountain stories. But if you want to keep a record of it, you go right ahead, preacher." Mary gave a small grin and waited to continue.

As he jotted down the things the librarian told him, Tom became aware of a niggling feeling, a sense that there was something she'd said he needed to focus on. The hair on his arms and neck started to prickle. *The knife.*

"You said something about a bowie knife. I don't suppose you'd know anything about what happened to it, would you? Did it get passed on to one of his children?" Tom had a sudden flash of his uncle Curry using one—had it been to cut fishing line, or rope? For hunting?

"Naw, can't say for sure. But I suppose somethin' like that would a been given to his only livin' son. The men did the huntin' and killin' in them days." Mary spoke as if informing Tom of things he wouldn't know anything about. "But they say James passed the black magic on to his girl, Rube, when she was a youngin'. She used to heal and conjure for folks even as a child. People thought she was gifted, till things went sour for her as a grown woman. She never had much luck birthin' babies of her own. The only one that lived was..." Mary glanced around the restaurant before finishing, "...tetched."

Tom's eyebrows rose, and he thought of Loy—and Curry. Family heredity? Family curse? It gave him a creeping sensation.

Mary leaned in and lowered her voice. "Somethin' wasn't right with that child from the start. She couldn't talk clear, never learned much. Ran wild all over the mountain. Then when she was about twelve years old, she took sick with a strange fever and died within a few days. And not a week later, Rube found her husband George sittin' under a tree. Shotgun in his lap."

Tom scribbled furiously in the notepad as the elderly woman talked.

Mary set her lips in a thin line and nodded. "Killed his-self. That one's in the record books. Suicide, clear and simple. Poor old Rube had to go on by herself. Lived a good many years. But they say she slipped and fell one day while she was up in the loft lookin' for eggs. Chickens ran loose back then, nested wherever they found a dry, quiet place. Some boys out huntin' passed by and found her hung by her own dress. Could a been there for weeks. Folks had taken to avoidin' her once her man and that little girl died. Said she'd conjured up somethin' bad and it wasn't safe to visit her no more."

Tom read through what he'd written so far and then looked up. "The Porters have lived up there in the hollow since the 1860s then. And what about the..." he hesitated, not sure what to call the thing his uncle claimed possessed him. "...the *creature* they used to tell about that supposedly haunted the woods up there? Do you know anything about that?"

"Oh, there's been lots a versions a that story. Like I told you, they say James was the one conjured somethin' up, and in the end, he died fightin' it. Folks say it ain't ever left the hollow. The tales go on and on about a creature that's stuck to the Porters, and that hollow, like fleas on a hound dog. Always been at least one Porter in every generation dabbled in some kind a devilry. Guess Curry's got it in his head he's the one nowadays."

"Hmm." Tom thought a minute. "You ever experience anything strange out there, Miss Mary?"

"Oh, I had my wanderin' days when I was young. Now and then a bunch of us would go up there and try to see what we could find. Thought one time I might've seen... somethin'.'" Mary fell silent again several moments, staring out the window with that distant look in her eyes. Then she sighed deep and shook her head. "Even if I had, I wouldn't want to go back out there again searchin' for it. My life's quiet and simple, and that's the way I like it. I'd rather be in church on Sundays with the Holy Ghost than go lookin' for evil spirits 'round every bend."

Tom nodded understanding. The conversation turned then to things like the new hymnals he'd ordered, and how Miss Mary still enjoyed singing in the choir though her voice wasn't as strong as it used to be, and the morning passed. But the preacher tucked the notepad in his shirt pocket for future reference. At least he had some further understanding of his uncle's motivation.

Still, he had no solid idea what they were dealing with. Did James Porter bring a scourge on the hollow itself by stirring up something otherworldly? Or was it that the Porter family specifically bore the curse, and without them, would it still haunt the place?

Then his thoughts went back to the knife, and a knot began to grow in the middle of his gut. Had the thing really been cursed? And had it somehow managed to be passed on to James' son and grandsons, and so on down the line?

Whatever the case, if the creature truly did exist, Tom wasn't sure any of them were ready to take on that kind of evil power.

CHAPTER 21

No more waiting for someone else to come to the rescue. It was time to do something about the situation. Yet, as Laura put the car in park in front of the farmhouse, she could feel the butterflies forming in her gut.

Duke greeted her at the door with a hearty *wuff*. He licked both her hands and worried around her in circles, panting. She had to bend down and assure him she was fine, rubbing his head with both hands, kissing him on the forehead, before he calmed down enough to let her move.

Aunt Hattie sat up from the sofa and gazed around the room. "What's all the commotion?"

"Oh, I'm sorry. I just got back and Duke was a little excited to see me." Laura sat down beside Hattie and rubbed her back. "Are you okay?"

The elderly woman looked up with a confused expression, hair disheveled again, crease marks on her face from the pillows. "Just... just got real tired all of a sudden a little while ago." She shifted toward the edge of the sofa and looked around again. "What time is it?"

Hattie coughed several times and Laura had to wait to answer to make sure she'd hear. "It's noon." Laura watched her aunt's face, her suspicions about the woman's health becoming more like fear. "Aunt Hattie?"

"Hmm?"

"Do you have a doctor you usually see for things?"

"Sure do. Haven't been to see him in quite a while though. Only go when I'm sick. Why do you ask?"

"I'm wondering if maybe you should go get checked out. You seem a bit confused these last few days. Sometimes that's a sign of fever, infection, changes in blood sugar levels..."

"Oh, I'm fine. Just a bit under the weather is all." Still she coughed into a dainty floral handkerchief. Hattie had the habit of tucking one in the waistband of her apron or the pocket of a dress.

A sudden surge of stinging tears welled up in Laura's eyes. She couldn't bear to lose Aunt Hattie, not now, not so soon after reuniting with her. Not while her own mother was out there in a cold dark cave somewhere at the mercy of a madman. She drew a cleansing breath. She had to get a grip. "Well, I can't force you, but if you aren't feeling better by the end of the week, would you at least call and talk to him about it?"

"We'll see." Aunt Hattie's answer was non-committal but at least she didn't flat out refuse. "Let's go get some lunch started. The sheriff and his men'll be hungry."

When Blaine Wilson opened the door, his dog went bounding off to greet him. Laura wiped her hands on a towel and hurried after Duke. Despite the nerves dancing in her stomach, it was time they had a face to face. She'd decided she had to convince him to take her along on the search for her mother.

He looked up from rubbing the dog's scruff and gave a slow smile. His eyes traveled down her body and back up, and a blush spread from Laura's neck to her cheeks. Her throat constricted as he held her gaze for several seconds, deepening the color in her face.

Finally, Blaine dropped his head, fussing with Duke's collar. "How are you holding up?"

Laura swallowed hard. "Working to keep it together." She had to be strong, had to show herself capable.

He drew a deep breath and stepped toward her, reaching out to rub Laura's upper arms gently. "I'll be heading out with a new crew when the others get here. We'll go over what they have to report and get moving as soon as possible. I—we'll—do everything we can to find her."

She stared unseeing at his badge, trying hard not to cry, his tenderness striking deeper than anything sexual. He raised one hand and smoothed her hair, but the fear and tension that had been building for days left her drained and it was difficult to think, or speak.

"You have every right to cry now and then. You don't have to put on a brave front for me."

She swallowed the lump in her throat at last. "I can't lose it now. There's too much at stake." Laura clenched her jaw and looked away before going on. "I want to help look for my mother. I think... I think I can find my way to those caves. If not from memory alone, then maybe, once I'm out there, the visions will lead me."

He tilted his head and raised an eyebrow.

"I know you probably think this is crazy, but I believe I have an ability, a connection of sorts with the other side. And I think it's more than coincidence."

"Laura," he stopped her short, "it wouldn't matter if you could read minds, raise the dead, and levitate. I can't let you participate in a police search. You're a civilian. It's my job to protect you, not hand you over to..." Blaine let the thought hang.

Duke *wuffed* and rubbed his nose into Laura's palm as if to show he agreed. She bent down and fluffed the fur on both sides of the dog's face as he licked her cheek. *Shot down again.* She knew when to back off, but she also knew she'd have to find another way on her own. He'd never give in, and she couldn't give up.

Her aunt called them in for lunch. Ham sandwiches on thick homemade bread with swiss cheese and butter, and large stoneware bowls of vegetable soup on the side. The woman never let a person leave hungry, no matter how sick or tired she was herself. Laura got up to clear the table when they were done, but Hattie shooed her off to talk with Blaine before he left to search for Robey.

"Walk with me?" He reached a hand out to Laura and she hesitated before taking it, still a little irritated with him for shutting her down. Yet, she found herself thinking how much she was beginning to enjoy this familiarity. They slipped by the men gathered around the vehicles in the yard and he led her out past the tobacco shed.

Blaine gave a crooked grin. "We don't get much privacy, do we?"

"There's so much going on." She looked away, a slight tinge staining her cheeks.

He stopped under an old oak tree, its bright yellow leaves casting a soft glow around them. The sun created mottled patterns of light through its branches as he dropped her hand and turned toward her. "I hope, when this is all over..." he sighed, "...when things are better and your mother is found safe..." He shook his head and looked away.

Duke came bounding toward them, breaking the spell.

"Okay, boy." He rubbed the dog's head. "The team must be ready. I'll walk you back to the house."

With lunch over and preparations made for the afternoon search effort, Laura stood in the doorway behind the newly repaired screen staring at nothing in particular as they left, worrying again when and how they'd find her mother. At the same time, a flutter in her stomach reminded her how Blaine's touch had made her feel.

CHAPTER 22

The creature stood upright. Easily eight or nine feet tall with long thick arms and huge biceps, its massive hands ended in claw-like fingernails, its canine teeth long and curved, its upper legs three times as thick as most men's. Its chest and shoulders were broad and muscular, its coat long and smooth, more like hair than fur. Sensuous in its ferocity, the creature's yellow eyes glared hard.

The artist's rendering Laura found on her laptop was the closest thing to what she'd seen in her visions—though she had to admit the real thing wasn't quite as massive as this beast. This one looked like a body builder on steroids. The real thing was large, yes, but not like the enormous specimen on her screen. Nor was it so sultry or shapely. The creature she'd seen was angular, harder looking, like something fed well enough but not overfed; like a thoroughbred in training, sinewy and lean.

The real thing? Had she reached the point she now accepted the existence of such a creature without doubt? This was just a picture of a painting, yet it sent a shiver through her. She'd seen the other one, the real one, close up, smelled its stink and felt its hot breath. Yes, she was convinced.

Yet the creature she'd witnessed had been ganglier, wiry haired and more menacing, less sensual, more animal. *Oh God, my mother is out there with that thing.*

Knock, knock, knock. Laura jumped at the sudden noise. Then she scoffed at herself. *Demons don't come rapping on the front door for a visit.* Still she took a peek between the curtains before reaching for the knob.

"Hey, little sister." Tom smiled big and wrapped her in a hug before she could respond.

"Tom!" Heart still thumping on adrenaline, she exhaled his name. Then she looked up at him, hand on her chest. "You probably took ten years off my life."

"Sorry, I was heading home and thought I'd stop and see how you and Hattie are doing."

"Oh." Laura took a cleansing breath. "We're okay, I guess." She paused. "No, you know what? We're not." They sat down at the kitchen table and she pushed her laptop aside on an angle. "I've been researching these." She gestured toward the picture of the beast.

"I warned you about getting too involved. It's strange how it wears on your nerves and your imagination." Tom grimaced before going on. "It's like the very air in the room gets thick, harder to breathe."

She stared without focusing on anything, biting her lip in silence. Finally, she spoke. "It's more than that. Aunt Hattie's not herself. She's acting confused and extra tired and weak. My mother's alone out there in the cold with a madman. And I keep seeing... those eyes. I just keep picturing the eyes."

"That was a pretty gruesome thing to find crashed on the porch. It's understandable."

Laura's distant look disappeared and she turned her attention to Tom once again. "No, not those. The eyes of the girls in my visions. They keep pleading for me to—I'm not sure what they want exactly." She paused and took a deep breath. "I think maybe they're trying to lead me to find what's left of them. To bring them some kind of justice, or peace. I need to find a way to communicate with them, get them to appear when I want them to."

"Whoa-ho-ho-ho, hold on there." He raised a hand and leaned back. "I'm sure nothing good has ever come from following that kind of vision, or dream, or whatever. That would just be plain crazy. You could end up falling right into Curry's trap yourself."

"Maybe, but my mother's in that trap," Laura argued. "If nothing else, I need to get to her, let her know—I don't know—that I love her and I'd do anything to save her?" She shook her head.

"We haven't had the best relationship, but we've been trying since—since Glen died and everything came out."

"Listen, I'm sure it's hard for you to sit around waiting all the time, but please be patient. The sheriff and his men will find her. You'll only compound the problem if you get yourself in trouble."

Laura knew Tom was just being logical but she didn't care about her own safety. If she didn't do something soon, her uncle wouldn't be patient about not harming her mother. He—and that beast—wanted Laura. She could sense it, feel it in her very skin when she'd met the creature's eyes. She'd surrender to the demon itself right now if he'd give her mother up. Laura only hoped she could find a way to get Robey out before walking into Curry's lair, because she was pretty sure she wouldn't walk out alive.

Laura's whole body deflated as she sighed. "I know. I know. It's just hard to sit by and do nothing." She knew when to stop arguing, and start planning.

Tom's face relaxed, apparently convinced she'd accepted his advice.

Laura decided to let him believe what he wanted. "So, what are you really doing here? I know you weren't just in the neighborhood. It's out of your way to come here from pretty much anywhere."

He pressed his mouth shut as he sought her face. Seconds passed. "Okay. I guess it can't do any more harm than what you've already found."

She raised an eyebrow. "You've discovered something?"

"I did some more research of my own. Supposedly there is a demon known as a ghoul that takes the form of other creatures. Like wolves. And it preys on the innocent, and the weak. Lures them somewhere secluded and..." Tom paused, sighing deep before continuing, "...eats them, according to the website. Not sure, but it looked a bit like your description of Curry when he changed. Though not the huge beast in that picture." He pointed at the laptop right before the screen went to sleep. "Thing is, I've heard a lot of descriptions of this something that's supposedly roamed the hollow over the years. And they all sound a lot like your creature."

Laura shifted forward and crossed her forearms on the table, giving her brother an 'I told you so' look.

"Hold on." He held up a hand. "I'm just saying, it fit so well with the stories, I decided to talk to someone I was sure would know more. More of the history of the hollow, and the Porter family, in particular. Mary Higgins volunteers at the Ashe County Library. The woman's in her nineties and she's lived right here in the area all her life."

Laura's eyes were riveted on the preacher now, her mouth slightly open, spellbound.

"I visited with her earlier. She shared a lot of stuff I never knew. Like the fact that Rube Hadley—you know, the lady who was found dead in the porch rafters of the Hadley Cabin?—well... Rube was a Porter. The daughter of James Porter, our—"

"—great, great grandfather," she finished his sentence.

"Who've you been talking to?"

"Our grandmother." Laura handed him the picture Beulah had given her. "She seemed reluctant to talk about him. And I think, a little surprised that photo was there in her family album." She watched her brother's face as he studied the black and white. "She seemed relieved to be rid of it."

Tom turned the photo over and back, taking several long moments to examine it. "Scary looking fella."

Laura raised her eyebrows, her mouth twisted in agreement.

"He sure looks white enough to me." He glanced up at Laura but she only nodded. "Sorry. Miss Mary claimed he was the half-breed son of a negro slave and her white master—a man by the name of Delaney."

Laura added, "Yea, Granny told me that too. And how he married our great, great grandmother before anyone knew about it."

It was Tom's turn to nod. "Yes, but did she tell you that his mother practiced hoodoo?"

Laura drew her brows and shook her head.

"It was brought here with the slaves from Africa where it was called 'Ggbo.' We knew it as conjuring, or root doctoring. James' momma taught him everything she knew apparently. Then he supposedly used it to call up spirits to curse the people who didn't like him."

Laura's eyes were wide. "Do you mean Voodoo?"

"No, I checked into that. They're not the same, Voodoo is actually a religion with leaders and established practices. Hoodoo is folk magic learned and passed along to their children over generations. It involves the use of plants and spiritualism to cure ailments of all kinds, or to curse a person's—or an entire family's— enemies. A lot of people who practiced hoodoo were Roman Catholics. They often invoked the power of the spirits using Catholic saints while Voodoo practitioners used ancient African gods and deities."

Laura's expression was grave when she responded. "I guess that would explain a lot."

"People say that in the end, whatever James conjured up turned on him. They found him dead outside his cabin, cut and torn to shreds, according to Miss Mary. Clutching a knife. Wait!" Tom snatched up the old black and white. "*That* knife... I'd bet..." He pointed to the blade James Porter held so oddly in the photo. He stared at the old black and white several seconds before continuing. "I never wanted to pursue this to its end. I'd hoped I could help our father without getting too deeply into the gory details." He shook his head, looking up into Laura's eyes. "I should have known there was more to all this."

She returned his gaze. "You think this... this *creature* is the same thing James conjured up back in the 1800s?"

He nodded. "Could be. And the knife, I think it may still be around too. What if it got passed along through the men in the family and Curry ended up with it?" Tom looked like a man struggling for words. "I mean, if this is real—and that's a big *if*. But if there really is a demon possessing him, couldn't it have used the knife to channel Curry's already twisted nature? Or maybe it was just growing up in the hollow with all that influence? Mary said there were other family members people used to claim had the power to conjure things up. The Porter family curse, you could call it, must have started with James Delaney Porter."

Laura sat back in her chair with a sigh.

Aunt Hattie entered the kitchen at that moment, her hair up and wearing a clean dress. No trace of the confusion from earlier, but she still looked pale and tired.

"Pastor Honeywell. Sure is nice to see you here. Sorry I missed service this week. Little under the weather, but I'm doin' fine now."

"Glad to hear it, Miss Hattie. I admit, I was a little worried about you. You need to take more care. Can't be climbing around barns like a young chick these days." Tom grinned at her, wrapping her in that big bear hug of his.

"Oh, don't *you* go fussin' over me too. Guess I can still take care a myself just fine." She gave a slight disgruntled frown and pushed him away, then went right into mothering mode. "You had any lunch yet? I can rustle somethin' up for you."

"No thank you, ma'am. I had a late breakfast at the diner in West Jefferson with Mary Higgins."

"Oh, Miss Mary. Bless my soul, I haven't visited her in ages. I need to get out and about more often. Losin' touch with friends and neighbors since I don't drive much anymore."

"Yes, ma'am. Well maybe one day soon Laura here can take you out. Maybe bring you to church again this Sunday too?"

Laura looked up as he spoke. Not sure where she'd be by then if her plans took shape, she decided not to commit. "I don't think I could bring myself to socialize right now," Laura said. "Not with my mother still missing."

"Alright then," Tom relented. "You ladies do what you need to. Right now, I need to get home. Elizabeth's probably wondering where I am." He turned to Laura. "You call me anytime if you need to. I don't know what else I can do, but we'll definitely pray."

She waved to her brother as he pulled away. The deputy assigned to watch over the place stood by the corner of the tobacco shed smoking. Laura shaded her eyes as she looked in his direction. Then she heard the distinct sound of a four-wheeler roaring away off in the woods and the deputy snapped to attention, hand on his gun. *Maybe we should hire Loy to watch out for us.* She gave a small smile and headed inside.

CHAPTER 23

The evening sun sank below the tree line without any news of Robey. Laura stood at the living room window watching the darkness settle over the woods. Nights were chilly up here in the mountains this time of year, and Curry had taken her mother without so much as a jacket. She'd been wearing black dress pants, a lightweight grey sweater with sequined trim around the collar, and a pair of simple black flats when she disappeared.

Laura shivered and wrapped her arms around herself.

Hattie was watching television, nodding off. Laura waited anxiously for the older woman to go to bed so she could slip out undetected. At last her aunt yawned wide, extending both arms into the air as she stood. "I'd stretch a mile if I didn't have to walk back."

Laura laughed. "I'll get the teapot going while you get your bath. We'll have a cup with some cookies before you turn in."

A little while later, Aunt Hattie finally headed to bed with Laura promising to wake her if she got any news, though she knew that wouldn't be happening. She wasn't even sure she'd ever see her aunt again, but she couldn't let her fears show. Still, she couldn't resist hugging the woman extra tight. "Thank you for letting us back into your life. I'm so glad we got the chance to get to know each other all over again."

"Goodness, child. You talk like there was anything else I would a done." The elderly woman returned the embrace. "You're still my little Laurie Allen."

"Thank you." Laura choked back tears.

"Aw, it's gonna be just fine now. Don't you let yourself worry too much, Robey's a strong woman. She'll likely give as good as she gets. You get some sleep tonight. You'll see, things'll be different tomorrow."

Laura couldn't speak. She knew they would be, more different than her aunt could possibly know.

She waited another ten minutes, checking the front porch for the deputy several times. When he reappeared, she carried a cup of hot coffee out to him along with a piece of Hattie's apple pie. Then, satisfied he would be occupied a while, she set her plan in motion.

Earlier that afternoon, Laura had laid out everything she needed in her room upstairs: a pair of wool socks, jeans, t-shirt, a flannel, a hoodie, and jacket waited for her on the bed. A flashlight and her Swiss army knife were tucked under the clothes. Her hiking boots waited by the back door. She'd have to borrow Hattie's shotgun so she'd checked it earlier to make sure it was clean, then loaded it, and set a box of shells out on the pantry shelf. She was as prepared as she could be to face a threat for which she had no true measure.

The last thing she did was tuck the note she'd written explaining her plans between the salt and pepper shakers on the kitchen table. It wasn't likely anyone would find it till morning. Her aunt was a deep sleeper and rarely left her room at night.

Sneaking out the back door, shotgun in hand, Laura circled the big tree to the side of the house and found her way to the dirt road. Her eyes adjusted to the dim light of a waning moon. She waited to flip the flashlight on till she was out of sight of the farmhouse. It gave off an eerie red glow in the dark woods from the cellophane she'd covered it with to preserve her natural night vision.

She intended to make her way to the old Hadley cabin and try to pick up the trail from memory, picturing it vividly in her mind. She hoped Lottie and the other girls would sense her coming and appear. If not, she would have to trust her memory of the visions to show her the way.

The woods grew thicker once she turned off Porter's Creek Road and headed up the trail to the Hadley cabin. The little bit of clearing she'd done when she was here only a few weeks ago helped some. It was fall and the underbrush wouldn't grow back much till spring.

She came upon the Hadley cabin about an hour after setting out. The night was silent, no crickets, no frogs, no breeze, everything was still. *Still as death.* The thought crowded her head. A deer jumped out of the brush immediately in front of her and she nearly screamed. Wasted adrenaline stung her body, locking her fingers around the gun barrel and making her legs stiff. She concentrated on slowing her breathing. The time would come for the fight or flight instinct, but not yet.

Laura hovered near the cabin, peering into the darkness, searching, waiting. She closed her eyes briefly and concentrated on a mental image of Lottie Edwards, but when she opened them again, she was still alone. "Where are you?" Laura whispered.

This is ridiculous. She had no idea how to call up spirits, and she wasn't sure she really wanted to. The thought of intentionally summoning the dead to appear made the shivers crawl up her spine. She'd just have to find the way by relying on her memory alone.

With the adrenaline slowed and her mind focused, Laura paid attention to the trail. Thin moonlight filtered through the trees, and between it and the red glow of the flashlight she recognized landmarks along the way, things she'd noted in her visions—a large oak weakened by ants broken off and laying to the left, its trunk and stump splintered, a fallen down shack that lay in a heap, the stone chimney still partially intact.

She walked so long she lost sense of time. She checked her watch, 10:45. *Two hours?*

The trail seemed to go on indefinitely. She kept glancing around her, trying to remember landmarks, but the farther she went, the more she feared she was getting hopelessly lost. How would she ever find her way back? Eventually she noticed a large boulder beside the base of an oak tree and a distinct rise in the slope of the ground from that point—the same as in her visions.

She drew a breath and dropped to a crouch, holding it in briefly to listen, waiting. The shotgun lay balanced across her thighs. Years ago she'd been an avid hunter, along with her husband, but she'd never gone after anything the size of the creature out there. Still, if she could take the thing by surprise...

Something tousled Laura's hair, sending a tingle through her scalp. She turned slowly to find Lottie Edwards crouched beside her. The child's pale face shone in the weak moonlight. She held a finger to her mouth. Then she rose and waved her hand toward herself.

Laura paused, fear clutching her stomach. She was no psychic or demon hunter, but she hadn't come this far to stop now. The child nodded and waved her hand again, mouthing the word 'Come.'

As she followed Lottie, Laura caught movement in the trees around them. Nearby stood another girl, and further on more appeared, though she couldn't tell how many. Lottie led her deeper into the woods, away from the slope, winding up and down through gullies, over rocks, through thick underbrush, the others appearing and disappearing as they went. Laura realized they were slowly circling north again—toward the caves, she hoped.

Laura put a hand out to stop Lottie and the girl turned toward her. "Where are you taking me? We can't just keep wandering around out here. I have to find that cave." She kept her voice to a whisper.

The girl nodded hard and turned to point ahead where a clearing appeared in the trees. A circle of moonlight showed a flat open area, but Laura couldn't see much more. She flipped off the flashlight and crept forward, cautious of stepping into the open. She followed as Lottie edged through the trees around the circle and stopped. The child pointed again, this time Laura could make out the dark yawning mouth of the cave entrance.

She crouched by a tree and paused. Nothing stirred. Lottie and several other young girls stood by, waiting on her to make the next move.

At last she braved the clearing, dashing across and into the mouth of the cave. She slid her back along the damp stone walls in darkness. The little bit of moonlight available didn't make it far into the curving passageway, and she didn't dare use the flashlight. Then she rounded a bend and a flickering yellow-orange light appeared ahead.

She stumbled over loose stones, sending a few flying and stopped, holding her breath. A moaning response echoed from the cave. The shotgun poised in both hands now, Laura crept forward again, peering cautiously as far ahead as she could see. At last she came to the end of the path and stepped into an open chamber. The firelight created wild gyrating silhouettes on the walls, across the floor, and over the rocks scattered around the cavern. Then a soft moan came again. Turning right she spotted Robey sitting with her back against a large rock, her head lolling sideways.

Laura forgot about caution and rushed to her mother, dropping the shotgun to one side. "Oh my God, Mom?" she whispered. "Mom, can you hear me?" She felt Robey's forehead and face. The woman was hot and clammy, her blouse half soaked with sweat.

Robey moaned again and struggled to open her eyes. "No..." she managed a weak protest, pausing to draw a raspy breath. "Youshuldno..." She slurred the words as if her tongue was too thick to speak.

Laura worked at the duct tape wrapped around her mother's hands.

"Hez... com..." Robey tried to speak again.

Laura reached for the knife tucked in her sock when a blow to the back of her head made the room spin. Lids fluttering, she fought hard not to lose consciousness, but soon her eyes flickered and went out.

CHAPTER 24

Wednesday, November 3, 2010

Blaine and his deputies searched the hollow and the mountain forest beyond in sections. They left markings to guide them the next time they went out. He trusted his men. He'd trained most of them himself. They knew he expected them to be thorough, but finding those old caves was like looking for the proverbial needle in a haystack. He'd been a boy of twelve or thirteen, at the most, the last time his father had taken him out to that particular area.

As a law man, he knew how quickly details of an experience can be forgotten, or changed through reconstructive memory. The longer the time passed, the greater the stress they were under, the more likely a person's perception would become distorted. In this case, it had been more than forty years since he'd seen those caves. No wonder his memory hadn't served him well so far. He checked his watch. Robey had been missing for about thirty-nine hours and one thing he knew for sure—the longer it went on, the less likely they were to find her alive.

"Bring it in, boys," the sheriff spoke into his hand-held.

The sun had peaked over the horizon by the time he got back to find an unfamiliar car in Hattie's driveway. Blaine looked it over as he headed toward the house. Temporary Ohio plates.

Deputy Richardson wasn't at his post on the porch. The sheriff glanced around the farm looking for him as he reached the steps, but then Adam burst through the screen door.

"Sheriff!" The deputy practically shouted in his face. "It's Miss Laura, she's gone." He thrust a piece of paper at him as a young woman who had to be Tara Evans stepped up beside him.

The girl's eyes were red rimmed, and there was a quiver in her voice. "I found that on the kitchen table... after we couldn't find my mother."

Blaine read the note, but he already knew what Laura had done. He'd seen the growing impatience in her face. He could read it in her body language. His heart sunk. He couldn't imagine her finding the caves on her own when he hadn't been able to with a whole force of detectives. But if she was out there in the hollow, it was sure Curry Porter would find her. *God, I hope that isn't what she has in mind.*

Tara interrupted his thoughts. "Sheriff?"

He lifted his head to study the young woman. Same green eyes as her mother, same honey-colored hair, even the same general build, but that was where the similarities ended. This girl wore press-pleated pants with a matching top and blazer, and high heels. When she reached out to shake his hand, he noticed her salon painted nails and the smooth soft skin that, unlike her mother's, had probably never touched a hiking stick or a shotgun.

"I'm Tara Evans. I just got here a few minutes ago. Your deputy let me in. What's going on here? First my grandmother disappears, now my mother." The girl shook her head and bit her lip before continuing, "I'm sorry, I don't mean to accuse you of anything. It's just..." She sighed. "You have to do something."

Blaine reached a hand out, "Miss Tara. I'm Sheriff Wilson. Blaine Wilson. My men and I are searching for your grandmother and we'll keep searching till we find her. As for your mother, she's a stubborn, impatient woman and I can't lock her up. She made this decision on her own." *God, why couldn't she just wait for me?*

He paused, shooting his deputy a piercing look. Richardson had some explaining to do, but not in front of Tara Evans.

Blaine sighed. "We'll find them both. I swear." He waved his hat toward the house. "Let's step inside and get you acquainted with your grandmother's aunt. You're going to be staying with her awhile, I imagine."

As they entered the house, Hattie appeared at the bottom of the steps in her robe and slippers, her hair disheveled, a thoughtful frown on her face. "Sheriff? Good to see you. What's all the commotion about?"

"Miss Hattie, this here is your great, great niece—Laura's daughter—Tara. She'll be needing to stay with you while all this is going on. That okay with you?"

"Well, bless me, no niece of mine ever needs to ask if it's okay to visit me."

Tara reached out a hand, but Hattie stepped forward and wrapped the girl in a motherly hug. To Blaine's consternation Tara started to cry, hugging the older woman back hard.

"Now, now, sweetie, it's okay. You and your momma are gonna be just fine." Hattie smoothed Tara's hair as she crooned, but the girl pulled back shaking her head.

"No, that's the problem. Mom is missing too. She took off on her own to look for Grandma and now they're both lost out there in the woods somewhere."

"What?" Hattie turned to Blaine. "When did she—?"

"She left last night some time. Listen, I'm going to let you two get acquainted. I've got to figure out our next step. Miss Hattie, you just take it easy today. I'll let you know as soon as I can what we're doing." He looked from one to the other. "You ladies stay here and be patient. We'll sort things out."

He leveled his gaze at Adam, who stood eyeing up Tara. Blaine frowned when he caught the other man's attention, and nodded toward the front door. The sheriff shut it behind them and turned on his deputy. "You want to tell me how that little woman gave you the slip?"

"I don't know, Sheriff. She came out onto the porch just before nine last night and brought me a cup of coffee and some pie. Said she was heading up to bed and she'd see me in the morning." Adam's face reddened as he spoke.

"Never mind." Blaine rubbed his gritty eyes. "I'm going to call the station and get some replacements for these guys. When they get here, you organize them and send them back out. Have them start without me."

"I can switch with somebody, go out with the next crew."

No doubt the deputy wanted to try to make up for what he must see as his failings. "No, stay here and keep an eye on the women. I'm going over to Beulah Porter's and see if I can find Loy. He may know something we don't."

"Yes, sir." Adam's face fell.

Blaine headed for the group that was waiting for instructions, but stopped. He knew he had been taking his stress out on the deputy. He turned back again. "Hey. That woman's got a mind of her own."

Richardson nodded, but his face didn't brighten much.

After Blaine had debriefed the other men, Hattie appeared at the door. "You two come sit down to breakfast. You got to eat somethin' 'fore you pass out. You're going to need your strength for what's got to be done."

"Yes, ma'am. But if it's alright with you, I'd like to wash up first and feed Duke." Blaine glanced between Adam and Tara as he spoke. There was definitely a look on the young man's face.

Hattie drew his attention away and the thought passed. "Oh, for heaven's sake, did you leave that poor dog out there in the cold? Bring him on in here then."

When Blaine came back into the kitchen later, Tara was petting Duke, who looked like he'd fallen in love all over again. *Like mother, like daughter*. And Adam was eyeing Tara like he'd been struck with cupid's arrow.

Despite the situation, or maybe because of it, the young woman showed herself to be as open and amiable as her mother, and every bit as inquisitive. She explained how she'd managed to find someone to fill in for her at school and how sympathetic the staff was to her need to be here. Then she drilled him with questions, and she also took over where Laura left off worrying. As he headed out the door she followed him onto the porch. "Sheriff, is there something wrong with Hattie? She doesn't seem, I don't know, as sharp as she ought to."

"Laura seemed to think she was under the weather. Hattie's a tough old girl, but she is in her eighties. It's hard to say." His brow creased as he thought. "Would you mind keeping an eye on her? Maybe try to get her to sit down and rest awhile?"

The girl's eyes widened. "Absolutely. She's my aunt too, distant maybe, but she's a sweet lady. I'll take care of her."

Blaine gazed into Tara's green eyes and all he could think of was Laura. If that crazy uncle of hers did anything to hurt her, he'd kill the man himself—with his bare hands.

He slapped his hat on one thigh and headed down the porch steps. He'd lost precious time filling Laura's daughter in on the situation, but he thought it might help to pay another visit to the preacher before he went to Beulah's looking for Loy. See if he'd found out any way to fight this demon thing, if it really existed, or at least to fight Curry's self-inflicted illusions.

Loy rocked on his haunches and bit his fist. *No, no, no, no, no, no, no, not Miss Laurie.* He sat hunkered down in the tree line just off the dirt road behind Hattie Perkins'. He could hear that deputy real clear. Miss Laurie was gone.

It was all his fault, *all his fault.* He should've tried to stop Curry and that beast back when he first discovered they'd been to Hattie's. He had to do something—quick.

He slipped back into the woods and ran for the four-wheeler. He'd have to go home first and get Rebel, but he could find those caves again. He had no idea what to do when he found them, but he had to help Miss Laurie.

CHAPTER 25

Blaine dialed Tom's home phone and the preacher's wife answered. She told him he'd find her husband at the church. When he let himself in later, he found the man in the office at his computer.

"Sorry to interrupt your sermon planning, but I need to talk to you."

Tom stood up and pulled off his reading glasses. "Can't say I'm surprised to see you. Have a seat."

"Mind if Duke comes in?" The dog edged around Blaine and trotted over to the minister.

"Not at all."

The sheriff sat on the edge of the chair leaning forward. "Laura's disappeared. She slipped away on her own last night while I was out searching the woods with my men."

A sigh escaped the preacher as he rubbed Duke between the ears. "Good God. What does she think...?"

The sheriff rubbed his face. "Knowing what little I do of Miss Laura Evans, I'd say she just couldn't sit still any longer. Thinks she can connect with spirits that'll lead her to him, no doubt. She's not a patient woman when the people she loves are in danger."

"Damn."

In Blaine's experience Tom wasn't a man who cursed easily. "Tell me, preacher, have you found anything else on this idea of spirits? I need to know what to do when I find this crazy uncle of yours."

"Some, and I'll get to that. But I also learned a good bit about the Porter family history. Something that leads me to believe there's more to this demon thing than I was ready to accept at first."

Though Blaine knew Mary Higgins was a sensible woman who wouldn't lie if her life depended on it, he still wasn't sure he was ready to buy into the whole hoodoo idea. An entire hollow and the mountain beyond it haunted by spirits invoked by an angry hillbilly more than a hundred years ago? Yet, if he wanted to find Laura and her mother, he supposed he'd have to play this like he did.

"So, you think the whole Porter family is haunted by an evil spirit? Okay then, how do I find this thing… and more importantly, how do I get rid of it?"

"I know you don't believe this stuff, Sheriff, but I'm telling you, there's plenty of material that suggests that those who are open to it, can be influenced by otherworldly beings. Fallen angels, demons, whatever you want to call them, they exist in another realm. The creature was introduced to the mountain by James Porter and through the years others in the family kept company with it in one way or another. Apparently, Curry is the Porter of choice for his generation. The obvious one if you ask me. Glen had a conscience and I don't think Loy is mentally, or morally, susceptible to that kind of evil."

Both men eyed each other, silently for the moment. Then Tom got up and paced the room, stopping to stare out the window that faced the cemetery. "It's possible he channels the demon through the bowie knife handed down through the men in James Porter's family. If you find Curry, and you can get the knife away from him, maybe you could keep it from possessing him. But then you may have to deal with the demon itself face to face."

"First I've got to find him. I'm planning on going to Beulah's to see if I can get anything out of Loy."

Tom sat back down at his desk. "Yeah, okay, good idea. But you'll still have to deal with the demon eventually." He pointed at the computer screen. "This stuff can give you the creeps." He paused again briefly. "Some say if you kill the host while the evil spirit is in the person's body, you consign the being to hell. Others say it can only be truly banished by using a power greater than any man. Of course, there's a catch to that. The person or person's doing the banishing must have complete faith in that greater power."

Blaine took his turn to pace the room and stare out the window. The cemetery, a baleful reminder of death, made him pause. Sure, he believed in God. Life was a complicated, fragile, and beautiful thing. He didn't believe it could have happened by some wild accident. Hadn't he himself felt an inexplicable spiritual presence in combat? But did he have the kind of faith the minister referred to? *Complete* faith?

Tom broke into his thoughts. "It stands to reason you can't hope to banish something you don't even believe in, Sheriff."

Blaine turned to face the preacher. "I'm not saying I don't believe. It's just, lots of men do evil things, very evil things, without ever claiming the devil made them do it. I know, I've been to war. I've seen it firsthand. Some even claim it's their god that does." Blaine waited as Tom appeared to grapple with the idea.

"I see your point," Tom conceded as he leaned back in his chair. "What do I know? I'm just a country preacher. I deal in redemption, mercy, grace. I'm a pastor, not an exorcist. I help men rid their hearts of sin through forgiveness, and teach personal responsibility for change. I've never attempted to reach inside and *pull* the evil out of them."

Blaine raised an eyebrow. "And I'm just a country sheriff. I don't know anything about the kind of evil you're talking about. But I know I've got to figure this out if I have any hope of bringing Laura and her mother back alive."

"I've got to tell you, Sheriff, the more I study this stuff, the more convinced I am that my uncle has given himself over to demonic control. That day in his trailer, he came at me with more strength than any man his age could possibly have on his own." Tom studied his computer screen a moment, then sighed, "I have an idea. There's a professor from the seminary I went to who told of experiences with exorcism. He tended to delve deeper into his subject than some. I was thinking about giving him a call just before you came in."

Blaine turned back toward the window. "I don't have time to wait. I'm going back out there today, and I'm not coming back without Laura. If I have to kill Curry Porter to save her, I'm prepared to do that even if I have to face the devil himself."

Tom stood and came around the front of the desk. "Well, if that's what you're doing, I'm going with you."

Duke set himself between them looking from one to the other, gauging the interaction, standing at the ready to jump in and defend Blaine. "I can't let you—"

Tom cut him off. "If my sister has to deal with this thing, then so can I. Besides, I'm a Baptist minister. I don't have any holy water or silver crosses, but you may need someone with a spiritual understanding of this thing." He paused, staring Blaine hard in the eye before continuing, "Though I can't say I'm exactly ready to face down a demon, I can't let my little sister believe I'd leave her to do it without me."

Blaine hated to admit it, but he might need someone to back him up. He wasn't in the habit of letting civilians help in investigations, but he had no idea what he would find out there. If there really was some sort of spiritual force at work in all of this, a man of the cloth might be his best ally.

CHAPTER 26

They were in for the long haul. Blaine meant what he said. He wasn't coming back this time till he found Laura and her mother. He radioed his deputies, telling them to keep on the search and alert him immediately if they found anything.

Meanwhile Tom changed into boots and grabbed a jacket.

Blaine glanced at the preacher as they rode in silence. The man kept his head bowed, his lips moving in what the sheriff assumed was silent prayer. *Good.* They could use all the help they could get.

When they arrived at the Porter house Blaine knocked loud and hard on Beulah's door. A few minutes later it opened a crack and the elderly woman's face appeared.

"Miss Beulah," he said. "It's Sheriff Wilson, and the Baptist preacher, Tom Honeywell. I don't mean to be rude, but we need to see Loy right away, ma'am."

She pulled the door open wider, tilting her face up toward his. "Don' know where he is." She turned her head, her unseeing gaze resting on Tom. "Lit outta here a while back with that hound a his."

"You won't mind if we look around a bit will you, ma'am?" Blaine watched the woman's face, waiting. If she refused, it could mean Loy was there and she was covering for him, or maybe he was laying low and hiding out even from his momma.

"Well, no, don' s'pose I do, but I'm tellin' ya, he's gone. I'd know if he was here. I can smell him. Ain't ever been too clean and he's got that hound dog's scent all over him."

A search of the house proved Beulah right, so Blaine apologized for the imposition and told her they'd check out back before they left.

"Alright then, Sheriff. You be sure an' let me know if that boy gets into any trouble."

Duke waited in the SUV with his tracking harness on. Blaine unloaded and locked up his pistol and opted for the Remington 870 shotgun. He chose to go with the more powerful, longer range weapon, loading the chamber and stuffing an extra box of 12-gauge shells in his rucksack. When he finished, he let the dog out, and Duke immediately dropped his nose to the ground. By the time they neared the shed out back he was pulling hard. After searching the building, they started around the side and Duke's head came up, his nose pointing up the mountain. He gave several sharp excited barks and his ears perked up.

Blaine turned to Tom. "This is it. He's picked up on something, and I'm betting it's Loy's old hound dog."

Duke pulled on the lead keeping his nose to the ground the first hundred feet or so, then he stopped and lifted his head to sniff the air. Blaine stayed behind him waiting. He didn't want to interfere with the dog's process. When Duke dropped his head again, he had to hold him back hard to keep him from lunging way ahead.

The dog moved fast, slowing down only slightly as they came to several small streams. He'd pick up the scent each time after circling, sniffing the air, and dropping his nose again. They'd been going on for an hour and a half when the sheriff decided to stop and get his bearings. He carried topographical maps and a compass with him as a rule. Army training had taught him to be prepared to find his way in rough country, though he was comfortable in these mountains. Besides, Tom had fallen behind.

They'd probably covered about seven miles at the rate they'd been going. Traveling mostly north so far, he figured they were somewhere east of the hollow and were now turning west. Loy wouldn't have moved as fast as they were, but Beulah hadn't been clear about how much of a head start the man had on them.

The sheriff allowed a few minutes for all of them to get some water and catch their breath. Duke sat down but kept his ears perked, his nose in the air. He'd settled in to the search well, slowing down, taking his time when he got confused. Blaine was proud of him, but he wasn't sure the young dog had the fortitude, or attention span, for the long hump.

"Ready, preacher?" Blaine saw Tom had taken his coat off to cool down. Despite the chill November air his shirt was marked with sweat. He mopped his brow with a sleeve. "Take your undershirt off. Put the jacket back on over your shirt and leave it open till you cool off. It's all about layering, preacher."

Blaine had left his bullet proof vest behind and removed the lining of his own sheriff's jacket. No way could he trek the woods at this rate in all that gear. It was more important to find his quarry as quickly as possible, than to protect his own safety in this instance. Yet, always prepared and always layered with an army issue *extreme cold weather clothing system,* he had an extra silk-weight ECWCS shirt, and a cold weather emergency blanket in his rucksack if needed. He wished he could be as easily outfitted for encounters with extreme evil spirits. *An "EWEES" system...* he thought with a wry smile. *Wonder how that would go over with religious exorcists?*

The men set off once more with Duke in the lead, turning sharply west now. About a half hour later, however, the dog came to a halt. Nose in the air, then to the ground, he circled and barked. When he started again he pulled so hard, Blaine nearly lost his hold on the leash. He glanced back at Tom who had taken the opportunity to relieve himself.

"Better hustle, preacher. He's onto something."

CHAPTER 27

Rebel lifted his nose, his head bouncing in air, his nostrils working hard.

He'd picked up a scent alright. Exactly what it was, Loy didn't know just yet. The hound was always sniffing out something. But Loy was sure they were getting close to the caves. It'd been a long time since he'd seen them himself, but he had no doubt he could find them.

Could be the hound recognized Curry's scent, or it could be the creature. Loy stopped, crouching down in a tangle of underbrush and shushed Rebel to make sure he didn't give them away. "You be quiet. Or I sen' you home wi' a wallop," he whispered.

The hound dropped its head and gave a thin breathy whine, but there was another sound coming from the woods. It started out low, like a dog snarling, but it got louder, and meaner, and closer. Loy slipped a length of rope through Rebel's collar to keep him from taking off.

The beast.

Loy sat still, eyes clamped shut, holding his breath so long he almost passed out. Then he sucked air and his eyes flew open. It was moving away, its throaty growl less frequent and quieter.

That was it, it was time to find Miss Laurie, even if it meant following that beast right into its cave. It was partly his own fault she was in this mess. He should've been watching closer.

He sure wished he could figure a way out of this where his brother got shuck once and for all of that creature, and everybody else came out alive and well.

CHAPTER 28

Fire flickered in front of her eyes as she struggled to open them. She could feel its heat too close to her skin. The acrid scent of burning wood stung her nose, and another odor she couldn't quite place. She ought to move. She needed to do something, but she couldn't remember what.

Then Laura felt herself being dragged along rough ground, face up, but her eyes wouldn't focus. Someone pulled her by an arm and a leg. Her head scraped and bumped once, jarring her teeth. Consciousness kept slipping away from her.

When Laura opened her eyes again she was mere inches from her mother's face. She groaned, blinking away the fog. *Damn.* Her hands were bound behind her with duct tape. He'd wrapped her ankles in it too. She lay on her side on the bare cave floor next to Robey, who was on a blanket, covered up. There was a fire in the cavern on the other side of her mother though she couldn't feel much heat from it now. Laura had been stripped of her coat, probably because it got in the way of taping her hands. She still had on her flannel shirt and hoodie at least, but her body shivered hard despite the layers.

Finally, she struggled to sit up, her head pounding in reaction to the effort. She had no idea what time it was, or how long she'd been out. Robey lay unconscious, her face flushed. The cave was silent as a tomb. She only hoped it wouldn't become theirs.

Laura rubbed her ankles together, feeling for the knife in her sock, but it was gone, and so was the shotgun. She glanced around, desperate to find something to work on her bindings. She scooted her legs under her and pushed off the floor to stand. Her head swam. Her body swayed. She waited for the wooziness to pass.

Across the cave on a large boulder lay the skinned-out hides of several animals. She hopped slowly over to investigate. Squirrels—hours dead at least, if she wasn't mistaken. And no doubt the source of the odor she'd caught earlier. A pile of bones lay scattered on the floor nearby, including a deer skull with antlers still attached.

Laura tried moving her feet one at a time inside the duct tape but nearly fell. She had to keep up the awkward hopping to investigate the rest of the cavern. She soon discovered a shattered mason jar and signs of a scuffle. Sitting down cautiously beside the glass she reached to pick up a large shard from the mess, using it to work on the tape. Damn slow progress and awkward at best, she winced each time the edge slipped and nicked her wrist.

She hadn't made much headway when she heard noises down the passage. Scrambling to stand, and hopping fast as she could, she made her way across the cave and dropped beside Robey. She pushed the glass shard under the blanket with her fingertips before she lay down pretending sleep, head back, eyes open enough to pick up movement.

The fetid smell reached her ahead of the man. He staggered across the chamber, one finger hooked through the handle of a large jug, a mason jar in the other hand. Moonshine again. Curry Porter was notorious for it, but the odor that clung to him was more than whiskey. He stank of wet animal, stale cigarette and— she couldn't quite place the other scent. Was it... urine? *Animal urine!*

Though she couldn't see him well through half-closed eyelids, she thought he looked thinner, and older as he bent over Robey. He turned her face toward him, shaking it in his clumsy hand. "Huh. Okaythen. You gohead an' sleep forever, woman. Don' needya n'more noways."

Laura forced herself to keep her eyes closed.

"But chu? You, I got plansfer." Spittle sprayed across her cheek as she recoiled inwardly.

When she heard him stagger away, she allowed herself a peek. He'd retrieved the mason jar from a rock and lowered himself to the floor. Setting the moonshine to the side, he held up the smaller blue jar and tapped it with the blade of a long bowie knife. "Almostime, almos. Be here soon. Then we gonna carve 'er up."

He grabbed the moonshine and poured some into the other jar, filling it about half full. Then he screwed the lid on tight and sat back against the rock again, staring at the glittering glass.

Laura tilted her head back enough to check on Robey. Her mother's face was pale. She lay so still Laura couldn't tell if she was alive or... *No, please no.* She risked moving closer, touching foreheads with her mother. Robey's skin was cold and clammy. *I'm sorry, Mom. I'm so sorry.*

Laura stirred and tried to shift her weight to ease her aching muscles. Then she lay quiet, listening, wondering how long she'd slept this time. A shuffling sound reached her from across the cavern and she opened her eyelids a slit.

Curry was moving around adding wood to the fire and setting a rack up over top. *Time for breakfast?*

He shuffled around and came up with two small slabs of meat, skewered the squirrel halves onto sticks, and laid them across the rack. Then he sat down on the floor staring into the flames. Despite the obvious lack of refrigeration and the smell of the skinned-out hides laying nearby, it wasn't long till Laura's stomach began to rumble. Though the thought of eating what her uncle had thrown onto the fire made her queasy.

Robey hadn't moved all night, or whatever length of time it had been. No daylight reached the cave's interior so Laura couldn't be sure. She took another peek at Curry and noticed he looked better. He wasn't as haggard and weary looking. Maybe it was because he wasn't drunk anymore. Maybe he'd slept well. Watching him she decided to bide her time, hoping for a moment of opportunity to present itself.

When Curry pulled the meat off the flames sometime later, he sat back and ate it—all of it—himself. Then, when he came over to check on her and Robey, she pretended to still be asleep.

He jostled Robey and gave a "*Hmmph.*" He was about to nudge Laura when a low growl from outside the cave grabbed his attention. He turned on his heels and stood in one swift motion, then hustled out.

And Laura waited.

CHAPTER 29

"Spittin' image of your momma." Hattie Perkins repeated the assessment for the third time. "Can't get over it."

Tara couldn't help but give a soft laugh. Her mother was right, this woman was a sweet, old-fashioned lady with a big heart, who loved to feed you. They hadn't cleaned up breakfast long ago, and Hattie was already working on food for later in the day. She'd asked Tara to help cut vegetables up for the soup she was making, and to roll out pie dough. Tara had some experience with baking, though her soup always came from a can, or a restaurant, but she didn't mind helping.

"I'll take that as a compliment." Tara meant it as a quip.

"Well you sure can." Hattie leaned in toward the girl with a conspiratorial look on her face. "She's caught Sheriff Wilson's eye, that's for sure."

Tara looked out the kitchen window toward the woods, contemplating the idea. "Oh? What makes you think so?"

"He's right attentive to her. Seen 'em standin' close, her lookin' up at him. The look on that man's face. Mmm, mmm. He's smitten alright."

Tara looked down at the potato she was peeling, but her eyes glazed over and her hands went still.

"Oh, my goodness, listen to me. I'm sorry, dear. I know your daddy ain't been gone long. I was real sorry to hear about your loss." Hattie put her arm around Tara's back and squeezed her. "It's a sad thing to lose somebody you loved so long, but life does have a way of movin' on."

It did, Tara knew that. She only hoped that it would go on for her mother and grandmother beyond this situation. Her father had always been there for her in his own way, giving advice, helping with finances, teaching her how to do things like change a tire. It was still hard to think of him as... gone... forever. She couldn't bear to face losing Mom and Grandma as well.

With the soup simmering on the stove and a pie in the oven, Hattie invited her to sit down to a cup of coffee and some cookies. While Tara poured, the elderly woman went to the living room and came back with several albums.

"Thought you might be interested in seein' some old pictures of Robey and Laura." She sat down and flipped a book open. "That there's your momma when she was about three, I think."

The black and white photo showed a little girl with curly, light colored hair looking up toward the person behind the camera. She wore a sleeveless top with shorts, but her feet were bare. She held a small box filled with rocks in her pudgy baby hands, and a tabby cat curled itself around one of her legs.

"Wow, that's Mom? I've never seen any pictures of her this young. It's hard to imagine her this little." Tara's smile spread. Not so different from photos of herself at that age. "That's Grandma, isn't it?" She pointed to a photo of Robey. "But who's that with her?"

"Hmm? Let me see." Hattie scooted closer and leaned in. "Oh, that's your momma's daddy, Glen Porter. One a the few pictures I have a him." Hattie coughed and leaned back, shivering visibly.

"Are you cold? I can get you a sweater, or a blanket," Tara offered.

"No honey, I don't think so. I'm just fine." The elderly woman drew her eyebrows together and glanced around the room. "But where's your momma? She should be here. She got here a few days ago, I think. And Robey? Goodness where'd those two get to?"

Tara studied the older woman a minute. "I'm sorry, you mean my mother, Laura?" When Hattie didn't respond she continued, "She's missing, and Grandma too, remember?"

Hattie tilted her head and looked up at Tara. "But they have to help me with Thanksgiving dinner."

Tara raised a hand to feel the elderly woman's forehead. "You feel awfully warm, Aunt Hattie. Maybe we should take you to see a doctor?"

"No, no, I'm alright. Just feelin' a bit under the weather lately."

"Why don't you come into the living room and lay down a while? I'll get you a glass of water and something for the fever. Is it in the kitchen?"

"Hmm," Hattie looked up again, "is what in the kitchen?"

"Never mind, it's okay." Tara took Hattie's arm and guided her to the sofa.

By the time she found the aspirin, Hattie was out cold. At first Tara thought she was just sleeping, but she watched briefly, feeling something wasn't right. In a sudden burst of panic, she shook her, calling her name over and over, but no matter how hard she tried to wake Hattie, the woman didn't stir.

CHAPTER 30

Blaine hustled to keep up with his dog, letting the leash out far enough to give Duke a clear scent path, but trying to keep it short enough it didn't get tangled. The trees were thick here, the underbrush lighter as not much sunlight made it to the forest floor in this part of the woods. It made Duke's job a bit easier, which gave Blaine more confidence the dog was onto a good trail. He certainly wasn't slowing down. Duke had most likely picked up on either Loy's hound, or Laura herself, if they were close enough, but the animal's eagerness was growing.

The preacher fell so far behind, Blaine would normally worry about the man getting lost. Their search, however, made a lot of noise, and left a swath of broken branches. The havoc was unavoidable, no matter how concerned he was Curry and that creature might hear and be able to evade them. And it was only midday, so he wasn't as worried about the preacher as he was about Laura and her mother. He couldn't shake the feeling their lives depended on him finding them today, whether he caught up with their captor this time or not.

He also worried Duke might run up on Loy and Rebel in a rush and engage the hound aggressively, or whether he'd find them at all. And he couldn't be sure the dog wasn't chasing some other scent, like a wild rabbit trail. Duke had little training in searches for anything other than planted objects. If he found the source odor, and it led them to Laura and Robey it would be only slightly short of a miracle, but it was the best chance they'd had so far.

Thoughts of Laura's possible death drove Blaine harder, creating in him an unfamiliar sense of panic. He pictured her soft skin battered and torn, her honey hair matted with blood, her green eyes—gone. He imagined he could feel claws tearing at her flesh as branches whipped around him slashing his face. That's when he heard the pop. Muffled and distant, but he still recognized the sound of gunfire.

In his distraction, he nearly smacked into a low hanging branch, ducking just in time to see Duke disappear ahead of him and feel a strong hard pull on the harness. His mind struggled to comprehend what had happened even as the weight on the leash pulled him forward and over the ledge.

His body bounced and he fought to get a foothold. With his back scraping against stones, his right shoulder bumped hard off a large rock, and the Remington 870 flew out of his hand and clattered down the cliff. Momentum carried him downward as he spotted Duke also tumbling loose, attempting to gain his own footing. The leash had slipped out of Blaine's other hand.

Blaine saw Duke scrabble hard to the right, gain a foothold, and then bound left and downward to the ground only to disappear from view, running straight into the cliff face. His own body continued down the steep incline, scraping, banging and bruising its way toward the bottom. He was thinking it couldn't be much farther, that his wild slide would be over soon, when he felt himself go airborne. He dropped the last eight or ten feet in midair, having the sense to tuck and roll as he landed.

CHAPTER 31

Laura struggled to sit up. She felt around behind her back under the blanket and retrieved the glass shard. She kept a wary eye on the passageway as she worked. *Please God, keep him away long enough.* The duct tape was thick but it gave way at last, though not without leaving her wrists and fingers bloodied.

Wiping her hands on her flannel shirt, she freed her ankles and bent over her mother, cautiously cutting the tape that bound her as well. Robey's breath was faint but warm on the back of Laura's icy hands, yet she didn't stir. Her pulse was weak, her face pale. Robey might not make it out of here in time, even if Laura could overcome her uncle somehow. And she couldn't bring herself to go for help and leave her mother there alone again in her condition.

She got to her feet awkwardly, her vision blurring as the cave spun. Blood rushed into her face and she broke into a light sweat. Her stomach rumbled, reminding her it was empty. At last she found her balance.

If I could get outside, maybe... As she passed the big rock near the passageway, Laura picked up the deer skull she'd seen earlier. It was a non-typical rack, with four points on one side and five on the other. She grabbed the lighter side in her right hand carrying it like a cudgel, and crept down the rocky corridor sideways, her back to the wall.

A familiar claustrophobic feeling swelled her chest as the path got narrower, and the ceiling lower. A brief image of being trapped in this part of the passageway with the creature caused her to stop dead. She held her breath as nettles of fear prickled her spine. *Breathe,* she commanded herself.

She was about to move forward when she heard shuffling. Stones rattled, dirt crunched, and the little bit of light she'd begun to view ahead was suddenly snuffed out. Laura turned and rushed back toward the cavern, moving as fast as she dared, and made for the other side of the fire—something to put between her and whatever was coming down that passage.

In an instant, Curry Porter appeared, wielding the shotgun he'd taken from her, the bowie knife in his other hand. "You know how to use one a these, don'tcha girl?" He brandished the shotgun with one hand slapping the barrel against the scar on his neck where Laura had shot him before. "You gonna wish you had it now." He stood across from her, eyeing her with a sneer. "You done went too far, woman. You messed around in things that weren't none a your business, and *he* found out about you. So, you see, I had to bring you back. You's a Porter, and now you owe 'im, and you gonna pay."

As he spoke, a large dark form emerged crawling head first from the opening of the passageway, as if the earth itself had given it birth. The yellow eyes glinted in the firelight. Its wet snout glittered as it unfolded itself to stretch its head and neck aloft, one eye keeping her in view. Standing feet apart, arms held at its sides, it exhaled audibly in regular rhythm. Then it lowered its jaw and leveled its gaze, yellow eyes burning into her.

Laura's limbs wouldn't cooperate, her whole body stung with adrenaline but her feet wouldn't move. She didn't want to take her eyes off the creature, but she noticed Curry lean the shotgun against the wall, and something else drew her attention. Lottie Edwards stood off to the left, her wide eyes darting around the cave, and yet her uncle didn't seem to notice the child.

But nothing could have prepared Laura for what happened next. Her attention drawn back to the hideous beast, she witnessed the unnatural transformation take place and she didn't want to believe her own eyes.

The creature vaporized before her, and Curry tilted his head back and opened his mouth, allowing the dark Stygian mist to enter, sucking it down, snapping his mouth shut and swallowing like a hungry animal. Then he tilted his jaw right and left, and stretched his neck as it appeared to lengthen. His open arms and his legs swelled, extending till his baggy clothes strained to fit his limbs. He was taller, thicker set, and... darker... as he turned toward her. His glowing yellow eyes went red. His densely haired right hand still clutched the knife. Still recognizably human, but now something more, something far worse, something terrifying and demonic.

It lunged for her, right through the fire between them at the same instant something—or someone—landed on its back.

Laura staggered backward, bumping into a rock, and lost her hold on the deer skull.

The creature that was Curry, and its attacker, went down in the flames, but the beast rolled and recovered its feet easily.

Laura watched in horror as Loy rolled in the burning embers. "Get up, Loy!" she shrieked. Then she rushed forward, grabbing him by his jacket and yanking. "Come on, Loy, get up!"

He rolled free of the fire pit. Rebel bounded over to lick his face and hands, mewling piteously. Loy looked up at her dazed at first, then his pained eyes darted past her and he struggled desperately to stand. The creature was on them in an instant, grabbing Loy by the upper arms.

As the beast heaved the man aside, Laura lunged for the deer skull and swung it with all her might, aiming straight for the creature's head. Loy's body slammed into a rock where he fell silent, and the demonic brute staggered for the briefest moment, a bloody gaping hole in its temple. The force of the swing carried Laura to the floor, down to her hands and knees. Then Rebel surprised her with a vicious snarl and went after the beast himself.

The poor hound didn't stand a chance. Laura watched in dismay as the creature drove the bowie knife into the dog's chest. But when it went for Loy again, she scrambled to her feet, glancing wildly about for the 12-gauge.

She swung around to find Lottie standing nearby, pointing at the shotgun that now lay on the floor at Laura's feet. She gaped at the girl for a moment, then grabbed the weapon and turned on the beast.

Intent on its prey with a heated fury, the demon thing that was Curry paid no attention as Laura chambered a round in the 12-gauge. With the skill of a hunter, she squared her upper body and planted the shotgun butt against the meaty flesh below the collar bone of her right shoulder, and fired. At less than twenty feet, she couldn't miss. Accurate, with a deadly precision belying her size and appearance, the round went into the kidney and the beast gave an upright jolt, dropping Loy's limp body. It turned slowly, red eyes going yellow, then grey. The creature took several steps toward her and went down even as Laura stumbled backward over the rocks at her feet.

She could normally handle the recoil of a shotgun. But besides being weakened with cold and hunger, in the rush of fear and confusion she hadn't been careful of her footing. Landing hard on her bottom, hands scraping stone, she got the wind knocked out of her. She was struggling to get her breath and stand when the evil brute stirred, raising itself to its knees and front claws. Laura's mouth fell open. Her head followed the rise of the beast as it stood again to full height and stretched its thick neck. Then the red fire emanated from its eyes once more as it lowered itself into a crouch, preparing to launch its massive body at her, flexing its clawed fingers, licking its glittering fangs.

At that instant, Laura heard a primordial scream, something that came from the depths of the worst terror man had ever known. It took a few seconds to realize the sound was coming from her own throat. She continued to scramble backward, slamming into rocks and bumping along the hard floor.

She realized she'd backed into the large boulder near the passageway when over her head flew a snarling, snapping missile of fur. Duke came from out of nowhere, landing on top of the beast, tearing at its head and the back of its neck, drawing blood.

CHAPTER 32

A spine-tingling scream brought Blaine to his senses. He scrabbled to his feet, rubbing his hands on his pants. He was skinned and bruised, but nothing was broken. He took a few seconds to scope the area in hopes of finding the Remington, but it was no use. There wasn't time. He bolted into the cave in a fool's rush.

Duke was locked in battle with something primeval. A large, muscular wolf-like thing with long arms and thick legs was grasping at the dog with hands that ended in long, sharp claws. It was clear Duke would end up on the worst end of the fight if Blaine didn't do something quick.

He spun around the cave looking for anything to use as a weapon and spotted Loy's hound with a long knife handle sticking out of its chest. He noted Loy laying still and pale on the floor not far away, and Laura, thankfully alive, backed up against a large rock. On the other side of the scuffle lay a shotgun, but to get to it, he'd have to go around the pair.

He lunged for the knife instead and tackled the beast, at the same instant Duke yelped. The vicious man-animal had sunk its sharp claws into the dog's side and threw him away like a rag doll. Blaine seized the opportunity to drive the knife home, as near to the kidney as he could guess, and twisted, trying to do as much damage as possible. The thing howled and started thrashing.

Blaine held onto the knife hilt with brute force, yanking it back out as the beast grabbed him with those lethal claws, digging into his left thigh and pulling him off. Despite the burning pain in his leg, the sheriff rolled and came back up on his feet, charging the thing again. He managed to grab it around the neck this time with one arm and came down with the knife into its side, repeatedly stabbing at it with all his strength.

Finally, he drove the blade into the beast's left flank, high up under the arm, shoving deep and hard, aiming for what in a man would be the heart. He held on, determined not to let go, though the thing was more than a foot taller and outweighed him by at least fifty pounds.

Then, Blaine became aware of someone calling to him. "Break away, Sheriff. Give me a clear shot." The preacher's voice sounded distant above the snarling, grunting melee.

Then the creature went down and rolled with Blaine still hanging on. All that weight came down on his chest. He was sure it was going to pulverize him as he lay beneath it, feeling lightheaded. Blaine was covered in blood, but so was the beast. He knew he'd wounded it but couldn't tell how bad. He couldn't feel anything but the crushing force on his torso.

A blast echoed through the cavern, and suddenly he was free. He sucked air and tried to clear his mind. The thing had rolled away, but somehow, Blaine still held the knife. Another shot rang out as the sheriff sat up and shook his head. The round had hit the beast in the shoulder. Blaine needed to move, and strike while it was still dazed, but he was fighting his own struggle to think clearly.

Then he heard Duke whimper and caught a glimpse of him lying beside Laura. The sheriff got to his knees and drew a breath, shouting, "Hold your fire! Stay back, Tom!"

Blaine raised into a crouch and shoved off the cavern floor launching himself at the brute creature, this time face to face. He found the sweet spot to the left center of the beast's chest and plunged the knife in so hard the hilt sank partway into the flesh.

The creature's fiery red eyes blazed, but its growl faded in its throat as blood spurted from the wound. At that moment, it was bent over so that their eyes met and Blaine stared into a depth so evil he shuddered. It was like looking into the pit of hell, until the fire turned yellow, then dimmed like a fading light and went out. The stone-grey eyes left behind were cold as the grave in contrast.

The devilish beast staggered back a few steps and this time, Blaine released the knife, leaving it where he'd driven it. At last, the creature collapsed and lay still.

Blaine struggled to breathe. He'd been winded and could feel the air trapped in his lungs needing to get out. He bent over, placing both hands on his knees, blowing hard. Blood seeped through his pants where the beast had clawed his left thigh. He'd have to look at it closer, soon. He'd slowed his breathing and finally managed to stand when Duke hobbled up to him dragging one hind leg and whimpering.

Laura was right behind the dog, her face pallid.

CHAPTER 33

"You okay?" Blaine looked Laura over, scarcely believing she was alive, sure he'd already lost her when he first spotted Duke and the creature entangled in a snarling mass.

"I'm okay. Bumps and bruises, but you're bleeding. We've got to get help. Mom's in bad shape, and Loy too." She spoke to him, but she didn't take her eyes off the creature.

"He's dead, Laura. He can't hurt you anymore," Blaine said.

Tom stood with the Remington 870 poised against his shoulder, still aiming for the beast. His face pale, breathing shallow, he stood his ground.

"I'll take the gun." Blaine put a hand on Tom's shoulder. "It's over." The sheriff eased the weapon from the man's grip. "Glad you had my back, preacher."

Blaine looked Laura over once more, assuring himself she wasn't badly hurt. He patted Duke's head, knowing the dog's injuries were serious, but he had to prioritize the needs. "Wait here with Duke." He looked Laura in the eye, trying to instill calm and confidence, though he was sure he was failing miserably. Her face was chalky pale and she was trembling so hard her teeth chattered.

When he started across the cavern, pain seared his left thigh and he nearly stumbled. Steeling his jaw, he managed to move without too much of a hitch in his step.

Tom let out a heavy breath and joined the sheriff as he checked Robey. "Is she...?" The preacher kept his voice to a whisper.

Blaine sighed. "Pulse is faint." His own voice low. "We've got to get her and Laura out of here." He drew himself up to stand tentatively on his bad leg. "You didn't find my rucksack out there, did you?"

"Yeah, it's laying by the big tree near the entrance."

"We'll need the thermal blanket and my other layers. We have to at least try to get them warmer. We can use the blanket Robey's on to stabilize her head and neck as you drag her out." Blaine stopped and glanced around the cave. "My walkie has to be here somewhere. I still had it when I jumped that thing."

Blaine made his way over to check on Loy. He couldn't find a pulse. He looked up at Tom and shook his head. Then he stopped to look at the creature again. The thing was huge. Its chest and upper body were thick as any two men's. It stood over seven feet tall and probably weighed 250 to 275 pounds with clawed hands twice as big as his own. Its upper legs were heavily muscled, its body covered in coarse brownish black fur, its stone-grey eyes staring into oblivion. Blaine shook his head and looked away.

"Devil incarnate," Tom whispered low as he bent over the creature and placed a hand on its head.

Blaine swore the preacher was trembling—hard—as he heard him mumble something else. *Praying again, now?*

"...Jesus Christ. Amen." Tom stood finally and backed away.

Then the sheriff turned and reached for Laura. Cupping her face in his large hands, he lifted it gently. "Can you help Duke out of here? He's hurt bad."

She finally turned, reality dawning in her eyes. She reached for the dog's collar and they limped after Tom as he dragged Robey to safety.

Blaine found the radio and grabbed the Remington before he left the cave and headed out to join the others. He called one of the deputies he had out still searching the woods and gave him the last coordinates he'd logged for where they were, and the best description he could give of the area.

After Laura, Robey, and Duke were treated with first aid, Blaine left them huddled together under the blankets with the preacher to watch over them. Then he took stock of his own injuries.

The cuts to his thigh were deep, and bleeding so bad his pant leg was soaked to the knee. The creature's claws had sunk into the muscle, ripping at Blaine to pull him off its back, and tearing gashes in the front and back of his leg. He'd probably need stitches. For now, he gritted his teeth and tore the pant leg open.

He cleansed the wounds with water and betadine solution, and bandaged them with large wads of surgical dressing and a few yards of 2-inch wide self-adherent wrap. Finally, he popped a few aspirin to help ward off the pain and inflammation and guzzled a bottle of water. Field medic remedies, but they would have to do for now.

He had to go back inside one more time to assess the scene while he could still move. Struggling to stand, Blaine hoisted himself up by grabbing onto a nearby tree. Clenching his teeth against the throbbing pain, he limped back into the cavern.

He rounded the big rock near the opening of the passageway and looked ahead, attempting to piece together the events in his mind for the unbelievable report he would have to write.

What he found sucked the wind out of him. For a moment, he was overwhelmed by the stench he hadn't allowed himself to concentrate on before in the middle of the conflict. But this was worse, far worse. What he discovered in the dark closeness nearly overwhelmed the big sheriff. *It can't be. It just can't be.* He rubbed his fists in both eyes. How would he explain what he saw there?"

Blaine Wilson took a staggering step. Then he waited for the wooziness to pass as he heard voices coming through the passageway. Two deputies appeared through the opening. The men did a quick investigation of the cavern, retrieving the shotgun, and joined the others out in front of the cave.

Then one of the deputies called Blaine aside to tell him Hattie Perkins had been taken to the hospital. Deputy Richardson was there with Tara Evans and the elderly woman, keeping an eye on them, waiting.

Figuring out how to get Robey out of the area proved a difficult challenge. But they made a gurney out of one of the blankets and two poles, strapping it with pieces of rope and gorilla tape from Blaine's rucksack and wrapping her with the thermal cover. They made a second, smaller stretcher for Duke with the extra blanket. EMTs met them at Porter's Creek Road.

Blaine left his men with instructions to return to the cave the next day to retrieve the body, complete their investigation, and report back. It was the best they could do for now. Tom would ride out with the deputies and join them at the hospital as soon as possible.

During the ambulance ride, the sheriff kept an eye on Laura's ashen face. She held onto her mother's hand in silence, not taking her eyes off the woman the whole trip.

He wanted to encourage her with the news that Tara had arrived, but since Hattie was now sick, he didn't want to bring it up. It wouldn't be possible to mention the one without revealing the other, and this wasn't the time. Laura was so small, so slight, and she'd endured so much lately—the death of her husband, then her father, her mother's disappearance, the creature's attacks, her uncle's abuse. Blaine had seen lesser things send tough, hardened men over the edge.

CHAPTER 34

Blaine wouldn't let the hospital staff tend to him in the ER until everyone else had been taken into the unit. He used the opportunity to talk with Richardson and discovered that Hattie had been admitted for a serious bladder infection, but she would be fine. Then, when it was his turn to be seen, he refused to be separated from Duke. The dog had risked its life to protect Laura, and had taken a terrible beating.

He told the staff, "You can put us in the same bed for all I care, but he deserves treatment just like the rest of us."

The doctor directed an orderly to put the dog on a table next to Blaine. "I'm not a vet, but I'm sure I can stabilize him and treat him for shock till we can get one in here."

As soon as the sheriff was cleaned and stitched up, he went to check on Laura. She sat forward in a wheelchair, bundled in a blanket and looking up at the monitors connected to Robey, her face pale.

"Hey," he spoke tentatively as he entered the room.

She peered up at him. "Oh." She looked as though she'd only just remembered he was there at the hospital too. "Are you alright?"

"I'll be fine. What about you?" He checked her over, spotting bruises and bandages.

"I'm okay." She looked at Robey and added, "Physically. They were afraid I'd go into shock so they started an I.V. I had to convince them to let me see her."

"Have they talked to you about her condition yet?"

She glanced up at him again. "I've been waiting, but nobody's come in."

Limping visibly now, he went and stood beside the bed across from Laura. With her doleful eyes on him, he had to swallow hard to deliver the bad news, but he knew she'd want to know. "She has severe head trauma. They've done what they can, but it doesn't look good."

Laura looked down at her mother's face as tears spilled over. He went to her side then and placed a hand on her shoulder, pulling her gently toward him. She reached up to grip his waist and rested her head on his hip. His heart swelled, and damn if he wasn't tearing up.

Tom slipped in at some point to stand quietly beside Robey's bed. Blaine acknowledged him with a nod.

A minute or two passed before Laura realized he was there. She looked over, her face clouding briefly. "You weren't hurt, were you, Tom?"

Blaine could see the struggle in her face to piece together the terrible interaction in the cave, but her eyes cleared when the preacher answered.

"No, I got there just after the sheriff here... well, I got there a little late."

A nurse came to change Robey's I.V. bag, and Blaine turned to Laura. "I hate to do this to you now, but there's more you need to know. Come with me for a few minutes. Tom'll stay here. He'll come for you if anything changes."

She glanced at her mother, then up at him, her face still glistening with tears, her expression wary. "What's wrong?"

"I'll explain on the way." Blaine wheeled Laura down the hall and took the elevator to the next floor as he told her about Tara's arrival and Hattie's collapse. He was thankful that by the time they found her aunt's room, the woman was awake and sitting up. She even had a nice color rosy-ing up her cheeks. He gave an inward sigh of relief, realizing he didn't know Laura half as well as he'd like. He couldn't predict with any certainty how she'd react to each new event or trauma and that left him worried, unsettled. He didn't care for the feeling. *Too vulnerable.*

The three women comforted each other, hugging, talking, crying. Blaine had the awkward sense he was eavesdropping on the emotional situation. Still he stood by, waiting till he was needed again to take Laura back to her mother's side.

As he watched her he realized, despite his awkwardness, he didn't mind waiting there for this woman. He didn't mind at all. And, he realized suddenly, he didn't mind if he had to wait for her for the rest of his life.

His thoughts were interrupted when Tom entered the room. Laura stopped speaking mid-sentence, her eyes fixed on the preacher.

"I'm sorry." Tom's features were somber. "They couldn't do anything more. She just quit breathing."

All three women gasped. Tara and Laura clung to each other and Laura reached out to hold Hattie's hand. The elderly woman shed her own tears, solemn, face drawn, brows pinched as Laura's body shook. Tara attempted to console her, rubbing her mother's back, but neither one spoke. Then Tom knelt beside Laura's wheelchair, and placing a hand on her knee, he prayed in quiet tones.

Blaine found himself wishing he could be a more personal part of the scene. He longed to hold Laura, to give her comfort.

At last, Laura choked back the tears, wiped her reddened eyes and turned to him. "Can you take me back down to her room?"

A few minutes later, Blaine wheeled Laura up beside Robey's bed and locked the brakes. She pushed herself up to stand next to her mother, swaying slightly. She took one of Robey's pale hands in both of hers and the sheriff moved away to give them their space. Tara, who'd gone along back to Robey's room, stepped up behind Laura and laid a hand on her shoulder.

Laura bent forward, tears running down her face, her body shaking with silent sobs. She placed her forehead against her mother's. "I love you," she whispered. Tara followed suit.

Mother and daughter hugged then, Laura burying her face in the younger woman's shoulder, sobbing uncontrollably. Tara smoothed her mother's hair and patted her back, consoling her as only family could.

Blaine couldn't help but wish he was the one giving solace. He had to shake himself mentally to get his focus back on the situation, but he determined then to make sure Laura knew how he felt—soon—very soon.

CHAPTER 35

Thursday, November 4, 2010

The staff put Laura in the same room with Aunt Hattie, and they allowed Tara to sleep in a chair between their beds. Tom had left late last night promising Laura he'd come back to take her and her daughter to Hattie's in the morning. But Blaine had insisted he would do the honors. The elderly woman would have to stay in the hospital a few more days till the infection was under control.

Even Duke had to stay the night on an I.V. to keep him from going into shock. Laura went to visit him in the morning as soon as she was dressed and ready to leave. He perked up when she walked in, lifting his muzzle to lick her face. She bent and kissed him on top of his head. "Thank you, Malamutt." She'd picked up on Blaine's nickname for the dog without realizing. "You saved my life. You know that?" A dark shadow swept through her as she sat down beside the dog. "*I* should have been there in time..."

The sheriff walked in at that moment and the self-deprecating remark was left unfinished, but her eyes swelled with the pain of regret. Her mother died, in part at least, because she'd made her uncle—and the demon—mad. She had exposed them both and they'd struck like startled rattlesnakes. And Laura hadn't been sensitive enough to the supernatural visions to figure out the creature's hiding place in time to save Robey's life.

"Hey, there you are. I've been looking all over for you," Blaine greeted her with a worried frown.

She looked up, tears choking any response, then turned away, swallowing the burning in her throat.

"How's the patient?"

Laura glanced at Duke, one hand kneading the thick fur at his neck. Managing to steady her voice, she responded. "They said he can go home with us."

"Yeah, he's a trooper." Blaine reached out to pat the dog's head. Duke looked up, eyes flitting between them, silent pity in his expression as he licked his master's hand.

"What about you?" Despite the pools in her eyes, Laura had noticed the gimp in the sheriff's walk when he entered.

"Just a few stitches. The scratches are deep, but there's no permanent damage."

Silence hung between them, both apparently caught up in their own thoughts for the moment. The expression on his face gave the impression he was troubled. She wondered what was on his mind, sure he'd be angry with her for striking out on her own to find her mother.

Then he crossed the room and stood beside her. Placing a hand on her neck, he slid it down to gently rub her back as his features softened for the first time since he'd entered. "We need to talk—soon," he said. "There's a lot to work out, but why don't we get all of you home first?"

Laura halted at the base of Aunt Hattie's porch steps when Tara stopped dead.

The girl's lack of motion held the small group back as her face turned suddenly pale. "We didn't lock the door." She glanced between Laura and Blaine as she spoke.

A small gasp escaped Laura. Her skin tingled and she took a step back, even though she was sure both Curry and the demon were dead.

"Wait here." Blaine laid Duke on the porch, commanding him to stay.

He reappeared several minutes later. Laura noticed him checking out the nearby woods and the farmland, his eyes wary, and the tingle spread as she followed his motion.

"It's okay," he said. "Let's get inside."

At the doorway Laura turned around, studying the tobacco shed and the garage, tracing the tree line, and the driveway. Would she ever feel rid of the evil that overshadowed Porter's hollow?

CHAPTER 36

The sun had sunk low in an orange-red autumn sky by the time Blaine returned later that evening. He'd called Deputy Richardson to come stay with Laura and Tara for the day, though Laura couldn't understand why. Still, she was grateful. He'd left Duke with them as well, allowing the invalids to recuperate together. He promised to relieve Adam by suppertime, claiming he had to go back out to the caves to check on the investigation.

Supper over, he now sat across from her at the table and rubbed his jaw with one large, leathered hand. A deep sigh escaped him as he looked long and hard at Laura, elbows propped on the kitchen table. Guilty as charged, by the look in his eyes. She couldn't hold his gaze. She thought she'd had time to prepare herself for the well-deserved lecture. Now she wasn't so sure.

Expecting the worst, Laura was caught off guard when his demeanor softened. "How are you doing? Really. I mean..." he paused. "That was a hard way to lose your mother. You've been through a lot."

"I'm..." a pale hand fluttered to her throat. She looked away and a fresh flood of emotion spilled over.

Blaine pushed his chair back and moved to her side. Then he clasped her arm in a gentle grip and eased her up. One strong hand cupped her head, the other smoothed the small of her back, enveloping her trembling body in his warm embrace. "I've got you," he whispered into her hair. He held her till the torrent passed. Then he led her to the sink where he found a dish rag and soaked it with cold water, dabbing her cheeks. She took it then with both hands and buried her face in the soothing coolness.

He pulled her hoodie off the hook by the door and held it for her. She slipped her arms into the sleeves and let him guide her out to the front porch where he pulled the rocking chairs closer together. Their eyes met and she bit her lip.

"You don't have to be strong all the time." He paused and looked away. "No one is." He spoke softly, almost hesitantly, like he was afraid he'd wound her with the wrong remark, the wrong voice.

"I'm not really trying to be. It's just—I'm used to dealing with things internally, you know? I don't usually break down in front of people—especially men." She stopped then, looking away, searching for words.

She looked back to find him peering into the forest beyond the tobacco barn. There it was again. That wary, searching look. "You haven't mentioned the investigation yet. Is there something you're not telling me?"

He looked back at her, a long penetrating gaze. "The team removed Curry's body this morning. They're still looking into a few things." He glanced away before he went on. "They found a hole he'd dug and hidden three other jars in, like the one you found here on the porch. There were several victims. The evidence will be sent away for testing, but it takes a while and there's not much to go on. We haven't gotten anything back on the earlier ones we sent off yet either. DNA records weren't kept until recently. They're not widely used even now—not in places like Ashe County anyway. Still, the lab techs should be able to tell us if they're human for sure, and if so, they may be able to tell the age at least. We'll try to match them up with missing persons files, but..." His voice trailed off and he sat quietly gazing up at the sky.

She waited. But when he didn't speak for several minutes, she pressed on. "And what about Loy? And, and, that thing? What happened to it? Is it still in Curry's body? Are they going to do an autopsy—or something?"

He lowered his gaze to the porch floor. "They're gone. Both of them."

Laura's eyes widened. "What? What do you mean, they're gone?"

Blaine drew a deep breath. "I went back into the cave while we were still there, and Curry's body was—different. He was normal again, except he was pretty beat up. Between you and Tom shooting him, Duke tearing at him, me knifing him, and whatever that creature did to him, he was in rough shape, but he was still an ordinary old man. And Loy? Just wasn't there." He drew one eyebrow down. "The old bowie knife was missing too—and so was old Reb."

She peered off into the distance, scanning the tree line, the field beyond the tobacco shed, the corners of the house. "My God! It's still out there? And now it might have Loy." She drew a ragged breath and a shudder coursed through her body.

They sat quietly for some time as the sun winked out below the horizon and a silent shadowy darkness settled around them. Any other time, Laura would have enjoyed the falling night, the waning crescent moon casting a dim, murky glow, the faint outline of its dark side visible in the inky sky.

She almost let the magic lull her, until an owl hooted from the branches of the old shagbark hickory tree, the second time in one week. It was silly to let old superstitions overshadow her life. Still, Laura couldn't shake the ominous feeling that thing was out there somewhere, watching.

CHAPTER 37

Friday, November 5, 2010

Blaine rolled over, dropping his hand onto Duke where the dog lay on the rug beside the sofa. "Hey old man, how are you feeling this morning? Think you can get up and take a little walk with me?"

Duke lifted his head, his ears perking up at the sound of Blaine's voice. He gave a soft *wuff* and stood gingerly, favoring his injured hind leg as he stretched. The sheriff threw his blanket off and swung his feet to the floor. He checked the stitches that ran across the top of the dog's right hip and part way down the leg. They were holding well, and the dog managed to hobble to the kitchen with his master in an awkward hind hopping gait. But he ate well, and drank a bowl of water. All good signs the animal would heal soon enough.

"You're a brave soldier, Malamutt. Jumped right in to save that pretty lady, didn't you boy?" Duke raised his head proudly as Blaine lavished praise on him.

The sheriff glanced up to see Laura watching from the doorway, leaning against the frame. She wore a soft grey t-shirt style nightgown with white trim piping around the v-neck. He traced the outline of her breasts and the length of the gown to where it stopped mid-way down her thighs. His eyes traveled to her smooth silky legs, all the way to the thick grey socks that came above her ankles, then back up again to where her hair fell around her shoulders in soft honey highlights, her cheeks still pink with sleep. He felt his face warm. *Damn.* He would have turned away, but the look in her eyes held his own. He was rusty at this stuff, but he could have sworn he recognized a certain kind of longing. The same kind he felt low in his gut.

He had to clear his throat before he could speak. "I was just about to take Duke out for a short walk. Have to get him moving, and I'd like to have a look around. If you'll wait, I'll help you make breakfast."

The brisk fall air filled his lungs and helped clear his head. He hadn't been in so deep over a woman in years but he knew he was ready for this, though he wasn't sure Laura was—yet.

Blaine made his way around the area slowly, patiently keeping step with his wounded pal, searching for any sign of the creature. It was still mostly dark, with a bluish black pre-dawn glow above the tree lines, so he pulled out his mag light to check the shadows. The pair made their way around the house and garage with Blaine flashing his light into the cars in the driveway as he passed. Duke was tired out by then and lay down on the porch.

Blaine went through the tobacco shed and out the back door. He crossed the field to a clump of bushes where a shadow caught his eye, but it was a raccoon. Its bright eyes gleamed yellow in the flashlight beam before it turned and ran. He'd headed back toward the barn when he heard a faint rumble off in the woods behind him—the distinct sound of a four-wheeler, one with a missing muffler. He knew that sound and was pretty sure who was out there. *Who else could it be?*

By the time Blaine entered the kitchen again, Laura had dressed in jeans, a white t-shirt and a blue and white plaid flannel. The woman looked damn good in just about anything.

She'd started cutting up potatoes for home fries and put coffee on. Blaine scrambled eggs and turned the sausage, stealing peeks at Laura every few seconds as Duke rested nearby on a rug, his chin on his paws, eyes flitting back and forth between them. *I could get used to this.*

The sounds and smells must have awoken Tara. She appeared at the door dressed in jeans and a long-sleeved shirt but her hair was rumpled, and she gave a gaping yawn.

Blaine grinned. "Guess we get up pretty early here in the mountains." It was just after 5:30, another two hours before the sun would make its appearance.

"It's okay." The girl talked through another yawn. "We have to finish making plans today as early as possible. There's a lot to do." She helped make toast and set the table, dragging her slippered feet softly.

Blaine glanced between the women. "I guess you'll be taking Robey home?" He tried to be gentle about the question.

Laura gave a resigned sigh. "After the cremation. It's what she wanted. To be buried beside my stepfather. But..." she looked at Tara, who turned away. "I'm planning on giving up my job and moving back here with Aunt Hattie after. Help take care of her, maybe find a part time job somewhere." She paused and shrugged her shoulders. "I've already got my house up for sale, and I haven't found anything to replace it yet. I don't know, it just feels like the right time."

It sounded to Blaine like Laura was trying to convince her daughter more than herself. He decided not to comment. He didn't want to interfere, as much as he'd love to have her this close. But then again, he worried about her being exposed to the creature, and the supposed Porter family curse. She'd already shown a susceptibility to the paranormal, or spiritual, or whatever you called the influences she'd experienced with the dreams and visions. He hated to admit it, but he had to believe the demon was real. He'd seen it with his own eyes. If that creature was still out there—and he had every reason to believe it was—Laura was still in danger.

CHAPTER 38

Sunday, November 7, 2010

Laura was packing her bag, getting ready to head back to Pennsylvania to put in her last two weeks at Hannah's Hope when Tom knocked. They sat at the kitchen table making small talk over a cup of coffee. After a few minutes, Tom grew quiet.

"Penny for your thoughts," Laura quipped.

He gave a laugh and shrugged. "They're a bit dark, and complicated. I have a visit planned to a friend of a former professor of mine from seminary." He paused. "He's an exorcist. A catholic priest. Blaine told me about the creature and Loy. It may be grasping at straws, but it's worth looking into."

Laura shivered. "Keep me posted."

CHAPTER 39

Laura hugged Aunt Hattie as they stood on the porch. "I'll be back in two weeks, the Sunday before Thanksgiving, but I'll call every day. You take it easy and let the caregiver do the work."

"Oh, don't you worry about me none. I'll be fine. Just wish I could come with you for your momma's funeral. Hate like the dickens to miss being there for you."

"It's okay. We'll have plenty of time to talk, and cry, and heal when I get back." She gave the elderly woman one last hug before Hattie went back in to lay down and rest as ordered.

Laura tossed her bags onto the back seat of the Toyota Corolla and shut the door as Blaine pulled up beside her. He unfolded his long legs from the sheriff's SUV and stood looking down at her. "Walk with us?" Duke was at his side, lifting his muzzle to nudge her hand.

They strolled along the lane that headed out into Porter's Hollow as the morning sun, and a chill breeze, flirted with the colorful fall leaves. Duke bounded on ahead. Thrilled at his chance to explore the woods he ran out of sight, then back to them repeatedly like a child unsure of his boundaries.

Blaine took her hand and they walked in silence a while, but when he gently pulled her to a stop, she yielded. "Laura." He paused and she looked up into his eyes. "I've been thinking. There's things I'd like to say to you. Things I want to talk about."

He paused again, and she bit her lip.

"What I'm trying to say is. I'd like us to get to know each other better. Spend more time together." He glanced away as he tried again to express himself. "I'm not always at my social best when I'm conducting an investigation, and well, I thought maybe we could go out. You know, date maybe?"

She hesitated, a gamut of emotions flickering across her features before she answered. "I'd like that."

"Look, if you're not sure, you can think about it. Maybe when you're back here again..." He looked away and she could tell her reply made him uncomfortable.

"No, really, I'd love to. It's just," her cheeks flushed, "you should know, I haven't—what I mean is I've never—been with any other man. You know, intimately."

His face relaxed and he gave a soft laugh. "You're a fascinating woman, Laura Allen Evans." And with that he leaned in to kiss her gently beside the mouth. "I look forward to getting to know you." He spoke in a near whisper as their foreheads met and he slipped one hand behind her neck and pulled her close.

Duke came leaping out of the woods with a loud *wuff*, jumping up to be part of the hug. Blaine usually discouraged the behavior but this time they both wrapped an arm around their hero. *A sheriff and a social worker drawn together by a dog.* Laura had to laugh at the thought.

They made their way back to the Toyota ever so slowly, with the sheriff holding her hand. Laura promised to call, and Blaine leaned in this time with a real kiss. One to remember.

CHAPTER 40

Loy Porter's eyes fluttered. They didn't want to open; they were stuck shut. He squeezed hard, scrunching his whole face, trying to moisten the dryness behind his lids. At last he forced them apart, blinking and squinting. His body ached like he'd been working hard for days, but he just couldn't remember.

He knew he wasn't a smart man, but he wasn't usually this muddled.

He sat up slow. His head pounded like somebody was swinging a nine-pound hammer inside, so bad he nearly gave up and laid back down. Looking around he saw lots of rock, and fading sunlight streamed through a large opening. He was in a cave. It was cold, but he was in a sleeping bag and there was straw under him.

Loy reached his hand up to the knot behind his ear. It sure hurt bad, but he was okay otherwise. He thought hard. The last thing he recalled was heading out with old Reb to find Miss Laurie. Then... He grabbed his head. *Ooowee, it hurts.*

He breathed deep and scrabbled to his feet swaying. The cave spun dizzyingly and he grabbed for the wall. Then he spotted a bucket of water. He drank some and doused the rest over his head, then staggered out into the evening light. He was on the mountain, way up from the looks of it. He looked all around and finally chose a direction and started walking.

After a while he remembered what had taken place in the other cave, up to the moment that demon thing lifted him in the air and threw him down on the rocks. He still had no idea where Rebel was, or what happened to Miss Laurie and her momma.

He was pretty sure he was going the right way to get back to the hollow, but he couldn't tell how long it'd take to get there. He walked on a long time before he stopped to take stock of the area. His breath came out in white puffs as evening approached.

As he stood still, he realized everything had gone silent. Then seconds later, he heard something that sounded like a wolf growling deep, and he froze. The prickles crawled up his skin from his back all the way to his scalp. Pictures flashed through his mind of a huge, dark thing carrying him through the woods. Images he hadn't remembered till now.

The lowering sun cast shadows everywhere around him, but his gaze fell on a large boulder as the darkness beside it expanded. In seconds, the beast emerged from the shadow, its yellow eyes glowing, steam rising from its hide.

It caught Loy's eye and held it, staring into his soul. His thoughts suddenly got all jumbled. It was Miss Laurie's fault that both of his brothers were dead. She pretended to care about them all, but she only wanted to do them in. She was one of those evil women who wanted to trick a man into doing her will.

But no. That wasn't what it was like. Glen and Curry had done something evil, and Cur had done even worse. There had been something terrible wrong with his brother.

The creature growled menacingly and Loy stared back into its face. *It's gonna kill me. Ain't ever gonna know what happnd. Momma? Rebel?*

Then came the black mist. It swirled and twisted toward him. He opened his mouth to scream, but choked on dark soot. Loy bent over coughing and gagging, until he managed to swallow hard. Then his blood burned as his body filled with intense heat. His skin stretched like it was going to split and he was sure his heart was in his throat choking him. Loy had never experienced so much pain.

He felt a wetness in his eyes and down his legs at the same time, and yet, his muscles swelled thick and strong. He flexed and glanced down. The ground looked so far away, and his hands... He turned them over and stretched the fingers out, staring at them. They were his to move, attached to his arms, but they weren't his thin, pale, bony hands any more. Then came the splitting in his head. He grabbed the top of it and held, twisting his body back and forth in agony. He reared back and let out a howl of sheer anguish from deep in his soul.

Loy tried to speak. Tried to cry out in his own voice but the sound got choked and the horrible howling overpowered him. The huge pawed hands tore at his chest and he fell to his knees rocking his body on all fours, thrashing his head, and howling till the sound finally died and he collapsed.

ABOUT THE AUTHOR

Yvonne Schuchart is a Chiropractic Assistant who once taught horseback riding lessons. She has written for publication in various periodicals and anthologies, including a piece on the loss of her three-year-old son, Jonathan, that won the Sparrowgrass Poetry Forum's Award of Poetic Excellence.

After raising and homeschooling all four of her other children, Yvonne decided to go to college at the mellow age of forty-nine. She earned an A.A. in Social Science while serving as a full-time Youth Care Worker at a residential facility for troubled teens.

Born in Havre de Grace, Maryland, Yvonne was raised with a fundamentalist Christian background in the Free Will Baptist denomination. Her father, who told her many stories of his childhood, was born and raised in North Carolina. The author draws her unique perspective on life and spiritualism from this personal history.

Yvonne now lives in the borough of Spring Grove, Pennsylvania, a community built around the paper mill established there in the 1800s. When she isn't working or writing, her 'other' life includes riding a 2011 black and chrome Harley Super Glide on the weekends, beside—not behind—her much adored husband.

 YvonneSchuchartAuthor

 @YvonneSchuchart

 yvonne-schuchart.com

 yvonne@yvonne-schuchart.com

ALSO BY THIS AUTHOR

Book 1: *In the Shadow of Porter's Hollow*

Laura's past is haunted by murder, demon-possession and broken family bonds. Can she save her father and free her family from the demon's influence?

Be sure to look for Book 3:
The Curse of Porter's Hollow,
coming September 2018.

Be first to learn when new books are ready!
Sign up at yvonne-schuchart.com